THE CAGED SKY

M.S. HUND

JEBESYL PRESS

Cover image courtesy of Thành Nguyễn from Pixabay.

Produced using Scrivener and Vellum
by M.S. Hund and Jebesyl Press
First Edition
WWW.MSHUND.COM

ISBN-13: 979-8842471362

For all the seekers,
be they hunting freedom or safety.

Shades of His Father's Sickness

Wil pinched his nose and stared at the gray sky. It hung above Harlebone School like a slab of stone, ready to fall. He remembered a shout, remembered twisting and his vision being eclipsed by brown leather. In that sliver of time before the ball smashed into his face, he'd both picked out the ball's stitched seams and wondered if it was real.

Then it had hit him, and the hot-cold splatter of pain had been like an egg hitting a frying pan, followed by the sharp taste of metal and wetness bathing his lips, dripping from his chin.

Those sensations were genuine enough.

And now the edges of his vision had gone gray and fuzzy. Cold ate at his fingers and toes, working its way up his limbs, adding to the general weakness that had been afflicting him for longer than he could remember.

This wasn't going to end well.

Wil's legs buckled and folded beneath him, and his knees crashed to the frozen ground. His face and knees stung.

"Not going to die on us, are you, Gravesy?"

A chorus of whispered disapproval greeted the question, a

chorus Wil hoped was real and not his ears playing tricks on him again.

"Poor form, that."

"Too soon."

"His brother, you know."

Wil blinked, willing the fuzziness to retreat, but succeeded only in squeezing out tears that dragged freezing tracks down his cheeks. Someone knelt beside him and pressed a firm hand to his shoulder, and Wil hoped it was someone real and not a phantom produced by his diseased mind. He didn't dare lower his head for fear that more blood would gush from his smashed nose.

Who could it be? He shuddered, thoughts turning to last Wednesday evening. He'd been certain he was alone in the hall outside the library, but he'd also been certain someone was standing behind him.

Shades of his father's sickness.

Wil had searched the hallway for several minutes, heart in mouth, wiping a nose that wouldn't stop running, trying to still limbs that wouldn't stop shaking, certain that his classmates would jump out to frighten him at any moment. It petrified him that someone would, but he was eager for it to happen. Such a blessed relief to endure a moment of terror followed by mocking laughter.

Just to know his mind wasn't betraying him.

Like his father's mind had betrayed him.

"Quit gawking, lads, and grab the ball. Restart for the Blues," somebody shouted. Older boy, probably a fifth year. "Get that nose seen to, Gravesy. Got a train to catch tomorrow, you know."

The hand on Wil's shoulder gave a brief squeeze and then vanished, leaving him clutching his throbbing nose, blood still trickling across his lips, warm on his cold skin.

The gray sky was so low it seemed impossible it wouldn't crash down on him, grinding him into the frost-rimed ground.

Had his brother's last moments been like this, before bullets plucked him from the sky and smashed him into the cruel soil of the Rangev?

Wil still couldn't believe that Ben was dead.

Six Months Prior on Lachfahree

Summer sat ponderously on Lachfahree, northernmost of the Cathermay-Gravence estates. The gray scar of water that gave the estate its name cut through green hills, and on its dull surface, two young men drifted in a weathered rowboat.

"You'd love her, Wil," one of them said to the other. He lay on his back, hands buried in a cloud of curly, golden hair, eyes fixed on the clouds.

Wil sat at the stern, grasping the oars, white-knuckled, lest they slip the locks and drift away, leaving the brothers stranded on the lake. His eyes stung with the pressure building behind them. The country air played havoc with his head this time of year. Nose, ears, eyes—all were suffering. The rest of his body ached in sympathy.

Wil sniffled, watching the wind push slow ripples across the water. He couldn't look down at Ben, couldn't imagine laying his head on the few inches of wood that separated him from the abyss below. The lake was a knife wound opened in the landscape, long, thin, and deep. Locals told tales of the monsters that lurked beneath the black surface.

Wil coughed, trying to dislodge the tickle in his throat, willing the sun to beat away the cold creeping up his limbs. There were already enough monsters haunting his fevered imagination. He needed to think of something else, needed a distraction. What had Ben said? Something about "loving her"? Was this the girl their mother had refused to allow in their home? Daughter of a banker down in the Smoke or something likewise beneath their station? What was her name? Why couldn't he remember?

"I still can't believe you're going to marry her," Wil said at last.

"What?" Ben frowned, one hand positioned above his head, thumb and pinky spread wide. He swooped the hand in a graceful arc, then grinned. "I'm not talking about Callie, you dolt. The aeroplane!"

Callie. That was it. Short for Callisandra.

Ben laughed, and Wil ducked his head to hide the blush coloring his cheeks.

Benwyth Cathermay-Gravence had thrice scandalized his family over the past few weeks. First, he'd accepted a commission to serve in His Majesty's Expeditionary Force to the ongoing conflict in the Rangev. It wasn't even a proper war, more of a skirmish between neighbors that His Majesty had seen fit to take an interest in. The Cathermay-Gravence family did not serve in such undignified affairs. Maybe if it were a proper war, but a mere border dispute?

Rubbish.

Then there was his volunteering for the new Royal Aeroplane Corps. Calvary, yes. Line officer, of course. There was historical precedent there. But the Aeroplane Corps? Grease-stained motors and patchwork canvas? For a scion of one of Saxe-Colraine's oldest and most distinguished families?

Of course, the military matters paled compared to the scandal of Ben's announcement of his intention to marry Callisandra Alandish before he shipped out for the Rangev. No matter that the Alandish family was a well-established banking clan. What mattered to Wil's mother was the lack of blue in their blood. They were new money industrialists with no breeding or history.

No class.

Mother had decamped from Lachfahree when Ben announced his engagement, retreating in a fit of pique to the asylum where their father dwelt. Hal, their oldest brother and acting head of the family, had forbidden the marriage. Not that Ben would listen to them. He never did. He didn't care that Hal would carve significant chunks out of his inheritance as punishment. Ben would always land on his feet. He was handsome, affable, and bore a storied name to fall back on if all else failed.

Wil sighed, wishing—not for the first time—he was more like Ben. His watery-eyed gaze shifted across the lake, worried by the rising chop, but needing to look anywhere but at Ben. Looking at his brother was akin to staring at the sun.

Why was that?

"You could sneak away from school for a long weekend," Ben was saying.

Wil fought the frown that tugged at his jaw, trying to keep his face blank. He couldn't let Ben know how much he wanted to do that.

"Nip down to the Smoke, Wil. I can show you the aeroplane, introduce you to Callie and her family. You'd like them. I can send you the money. Nobody would know."

"Nobody" meaning their mother and Hal, but of course they'd find out. The masters at Harlebone would report Wil's leaving to them, and some combination of money and private investigators would discover where Wil had gone and who he'd been to see.

Still, he couldn't imagine not visiting Ben before he left for the war.

Or the conflict.

Or whatever they were calling the troubles in the Rangev now.

Wil's thoughts drifted back to the fathoms of dark water beneath them.

Danger hid in those depths.

A sudden vision stole over him, darkening his eyes.

Not now!

Not—

Ben's hair straightened and paled to near-white. His face went slack and melted into Hal's sharper features. And then the amalgam of Wil's brothers was whirling to its feet, setting the boat rocking. It surged forward, barreling into Wil and sending them both crashing through the stern wall of the hull and into the water.

Splashing, sinking, drowning.

Everything went black and cold, so very cold.

"Wil?"

Wil coughed and blinked back to the boat drifting on the dull, gray water of the lake. The sun beat down on him, but it wasn't enough to banish the cold that had colonized his entire body, setting him to shivering. Ben smiled up at him, and the light in his brother's eyes and dancing on the golden curls forced Wil to look away.

The Burden of Your Blood

Harlebone School perched on a hill above the market town of Saint Malvern's Green. The school itself was a square of brick being devoured by ivy, enclosing a smaller square of cropped lawn and flagstone walks. A small fountain featuring the personifications of the six elemental spirits from classical Saxer myth sat at its center. Harlebone stressed the classics whenever it could. It was a place built on classical foundations.

Classical myth and literature as the foundation of education. Classical methods of discipline and punishment to reinforce standards. All to preserve the classical fortunes amassed by classical families to fund the whole classical lot.

Wil sat on his suitcase beside the fountain and prodded at his nose. It alternately stung and went numb, and he was having trouble breathing through it, though he couldn't be certain if that was entirely from getting hit with the ball yesterday. For weeks, he'd been suffering cycles of fever and congestion, weakness and chills. Or had it been longer? Had it begun when he'd arrived at Harlebone?

Or was it after he'd learned of Ben's death?

Other boys milled around, waiting for release, their breath pluming in the chill air. Only boys from the oldest families were leaving tonight for their midwinter break. Most of those whose titles only went back two or three centuries would catch a train south to the capital beneath its constant pall of smoke tomorrow, while the boys from the families of true quality would head north to their ancient estates tonight.

Boys like Wilstaire Cathermay-Gravence.

What a bitter mouthful his name was.

"On the nineteen-thirty, Gravesy?"

Wil glanced up at the older boy who'd spoken to him. A fifth year. Carcette-something? Father a duke, perhaps? The boy had turned his sharp features away from Wil, not caring for his answer. What an inane question. Of course Wil would be on the train heading north. Just as this Carcette creature would be. He was only speaking to Wil in order to be seen speaking to a Cathermay-Gravence, underlining that he'd known Wil's brother when Ben had attended Harlebone. It was a routine assertion of position and family connections, just like their brothers and fathers and grandfathers had done for hundreds of years. It was what their sort did.

Wil ran a tongue over cracked lips and patted the chest pocket where he'd stashed his tickets, one for the Saint Malvern's to Isleywich express and the second for the connecting local train to Brentham. He nodded, knowing the older boy wasn't looking at him and didn't care if he answered.

"Your attention, young sirs."

Master Hazelworthy rapped his cane on the edge of the fountain and waited for the dull drone of conversation to wither. Wil's eldest brother, Hal, had been a favorite of Master Hazelworthy. No surprise there. Hazelworthy taught mathematics and science, and Hal had a mind made for figures. Ben was a desperate disappointment by comparison, and Wil fell even further short of the high bar Hal had set. The master's pale eyes touched on Wil for a second, narrowing at the sight of the bruising around Wil's nose, probably made worse by the faltering sun. Hazelworthy sniffed and looked away. More disappointment to add to Wil's ledger.

The master cleared his throat. "I expect the older lads to help the younger ones. First years without an older brother, find somebody in your house to follow. Don't dally in the town, please. I expect you will all enjoy your time at home with family, but don't neglect your studies. Being away from Harlebone doesn't excuse the burden of your blood. You are the future of Saxe-Colraine. Remember that, and conduct yourselves accordingly."

With that last admonition, the master spun, dark coattails whipping around behind him as he stalked away from the main gate. Wil pushed to his feet, waiting for the customary flutter of dizziness to pass, and grabbed his suitcase. It was heavier than it should have been, though he hoped nobody would notice. Extra clothes and books he couldn't bear to leave behind filled the case almost to bursting.

His hand drifted to the tickets in his pocket again.

Nobody had to know that he didn't plan to use them.

Or that he didn't intend to return after the break.

4

A Shadow Lurking in the Heart

The pack of Harlebone boys remained solemn and orderly until the forest closed behind them. Freed from the watchful walls of the school, the formal rows disintegrated into knots of mock combat that sometimes turned real. Jeers flew, only to be volleyed back. Bags and cases swung in bruising arcs.

Uncertain shapes in the shadows beneath the trees and the chaotic swirl of bodies did nothing to settle Wil's nerves. He twitched at every movement, flinched away from every sound, all the while telling himself that they were real, produced by boys he'd shared classrooms and dining halls with for the past three months. There were no surprises here. Everything was real, not some corruption spat out by his diseased brain.

Wil envisaged himself as a shadow lurking in the heart of the melee, floating serenely down the hill to Saint Malvern's Green. Desperate for a distraction from the capering imps around him, he pictured the market town, using the map plastered above the Harlebone library fireplace as his model. Buildings clustered in a cross shape, huddled along the intersecting lines of the canal and the turnpike road. Of course, the library map was decades out of date. Not only had the buildings of the Green spread like mold from the crossed lines, but the old turnpike road was now a poor sibling of the rail line that shadowed its track. The expanding town had devoured forests and farmland alike, though its progress had stalled at the hill crowned by Harlebone School.

Wil blinked away the afterimage of the dated map, swallowing the lump in his throat as he thought of Ben looking at that same image in the library years ago. Had his brother imagined himself in the clouds, looking down at the landscape? Perhaps that was when the desire to fly took hold in his breast? Tears blurred the first lights winking through the thinning trees.

Wil's time was coming.

The time for bold action and escape.

His steps quickened, and saliva flooded his mouth. The merchants of Saint Malvern's Green were not stupid. They knew when the boys would come, and all the shops and cafes and bakeries lining their path would remain open late tonight, tempting the fledgling aristocrats before their long train journeys.

Wil yearned for a pastry and a browse in the bookseller's, but time was short. He had to reach the station early so he could exchange the tickets Hal had mailed. He'd memorized the timetables and fares and knew he'd have extra cash from the exchange to supplement what he'd already squirreled away for his journey to the Smoke.

The Harlebone pack poured through the outskirts of Saint Malvern's Green, and Wil felt the weight of hungry eyes, the thinly veiled malice and greed of the townsfolk. Some boys peeled off, sucked away by the promise of sweets or trinkets, but the main body flowed on, dragged inevitably toward the canal. This wasn't the direct route to the station, but it was the pack's traditional path. Their brothers and fathers and grandfathers had followed the same track down the centuries.

Wil knew he could plot his own route, a faster route. He didn't have to stay with the pack. But it was better not to be alone. Bad things happened to Wil when he was alone. Solitude and quiet bred monsters.

The pack slowed as it passed a motley array of boats clustered along the canal. Colored lights burned at the bows and sterns of long, narrow hulls painted in a myriad of shades.

Rivane boats.

Floating homes and marketplaces for the gypsy canal folk.

Why were boys always drawn to danger, to tales of abduction and magic, to the strange rites and practices said to take place on such boats?

"Time's tight, Gravesy, but where there's a will and some coin..."

Carcette was beside him, grinning and rubbing his fingers together. The fifth year glanced sidelong at Wil, who tried to ignore his presence. But the older boy sidled closer and dropped his voice, digging his elbow into Wil's ribs.

"Heard your brother visited a red lantern boat every time he passed through the Green."

Red lantern? What was that supposed to mean?

"What do you say, Gravesy? Time for a tumble?"

A tumble?

Oh, no...

5

A Little Curl of Nausea

Wil wasn't sure how it happened, how the trio of fifth years and their handful of younger hangers-on cut him from the main pack. Piping voices dwindled into the middle distance further along the canal, but Carcette and his cronies kept Wil from pursuing them.

"Not interested," he muttered, hoping they would let him go, but knowing they wouldn't.

"You've been moping about your brother, barely paying attention in classes. You need something to shake you out of the doldrums."

Wil blinked, watching Carcette's sharp eyes shift from Wil to the canal to the road they'd all come down. Was he acting on orders from the masters? Or maybe from Wil's own family? He wouldn't put it past Hal to arrange something like this. His eye twitched in time with the throbbing point of pain behind it.

"I have a train to catch," he tried, wincing at the quaver in his voice.

"So do we all, Gravesy." Carcette grinned. "But it's your first time, right? Won't take too long."

Wil breathed deep, trying to steady the trembling in his shoulders and legs. He didn't have as much time as Carcette thought. He needed to get to the station and exchange his tickets before the train left for the Smoke. The throbbing in his head spawned a little curl of nausea in his gut.

"I have to go," he growled, and stepped forward, hoping the wall of boys would part before him.

They didn't.

Carcette shoved him back, grin fading. "Don't want to pay?"

Wil shook his head. "It's not that."

"You fancy boys instead?" Carcette stepped forward, fingers closing around Wil's pathetic bicep.

Wil felt himself going pink and shook his head more vigorously, though he wasn't sure that wasn't true and sometimes worried about it. He could find beauty in both the male and female form, but that didn't mean he fancied either. He wasn't sure he fancied any sort of person. How were you supposed to know? Shouldn't it be obvious?

Wil flinched as Carcette's grip tightened. Another boy grabbed hold of his other arm, and together they dragged him toward a boat with a red lantern dangling above its aft deck.

"Let him go."

The voice was quiet, but carried a note of command that halted Carcette and his accomplices. Wil twisted to look over his shoulder at the woman standing behind them, silhouetted by the lights behind her. The hat and coat were Rivane, but the voice could have belonged to any of their mothers or aunts or sisters. Educated tones, clipped in the manner of a matriarch addressing her staff. But the way she was standing…

Wil sucked in a sharp breath. It was almost like she was pointing something at them. A weapon, perhaps?

"This has nothing to do with you," Carcette snarled.

Wil almost admired him for not quailing in the face of that voice, that stance, the possibility of violence.

The woman stepped forward, and the crimson light cast by the lantern painted detail on her silhouette. Her long coat was repeatedly patched-over in the style of the canal folk. The original shape of her hat had long since faded with age and wear. Baggy trousers flared from scuffed boots, and a wicked blade flashed in her hand. It was more a workman's tool than a weapon, but it could still prove deadly.

Everything about her said Rivane.

Everything but the voice.

And the color of the thick braid of hair that trailed from beneath the battered hat. Too light. Much like the eyes glittering above the scarf that covered her mouth and nose.

The pale eyes narrowed. "Run along to your train, little boys."

A familiar accent, and the threat was unmistakable.

Carcette's grip tightened, almost touching bone, and Wil gasped.

The woman stepped forward, her knife weaving a complicated pattern before her, and the first boy broke. Expensive leather soles slapped the cobbles as he retreated. Then a second broke. And a third.

"See you at the station." Carcette's breath was warm on Wil's ear, but a chill settled on his chest. His heart kicked hard against his ribs.

Then Carcette dropped his arm, leaving behind a stinging agony like a shadow of that iron grip.

More footsteps retreated, though they didn't hurry.

Wil stared at the Rivane woman who was definitely not Rivane.

A woman with a knife in her hand.

Beneath the roar of blood in his ears, Wil could hear the canal sloshing against wooden hulls and stone banks. He swallowed and wished, for the first time in his brief life, that he was imagining the figure before him.

Eighteen Months Earlier in a Crumbling Old Heap

The house had grown quiet since they took his father away, since Ben had decamped to the Smoke after graduation from Harlebone, since Hal had embarked on his tour of the family estates. It was just Wil and his mother and the skeleton crew of staff that had remained loyal through his father's decline.

None of the staff talked to Wil, and his mother would rather spend her time cloistered with her novels and her letters in her stifling rooms, enduring the midsummer heat like some sort of martyr.

Wil wondered if she felt the same way about his father's madness, if she relished the role of the suffering spouse. It was a role not so different from that of the heroines in her novels, women who lived in houses much like this crumbling old heap.

Sixty-seven rooms, mostly empty.

Save for the shadows.

Wil's gaze skirted the shadows, not daring to probe their depths for fear of what lurked there. Or rather, what didn't lurk there. Things his mind brought into being. Was it imagination, or the product of a brain slowly succumbing to disease? The same disease that had ruined his father, perhaps?

Better not to think of that. Better to comfort himself with lies. His tutors had both raved and remonstrated over his imagination, fascinating to some, infuriating to others. Still, they all agreed he was blessed—or cursed—with a mind capable of constructing worlds of air and dreams. He'd always been content to escape into such worlds before his father's decline, but now, when he knew what such escapes might portend…?

Wil paused at the bottom of a curved sweep of stairs, surrounded by emptiness and silence, dreading to hear a faint chuckle or whisper. Or worse, a distant groan or scream. Had it always been like this? Had it grown worse since the men in the gray coats took his father away in the windowless carriage?

Sweat pooled in Wil's armpits and trickled down his ribs. Dark wings fluttered at the edges of his vision.

Shapes in the shadows.

Whispering voices.

Whispering…

A Gloved Hand Stretched Out Toward Him

"You'll miss your train."

Wil blinked. The blade was almost liquid in the bloody light cast by the red lantern. It mesmerized him such that he almost reached for it before the woman made it vanish into a pocket of her much-patched coat.

"Your train?"

Wil's eyes lifted to meet those of the woman. The scarf wound round the lower half of her face muffled her cultured voice, and the fabric was expensive, not something one would expect canal folk to possess. It wouldn't have looked out of place around his mother's neck.

The woman shrugged and turned away.

"Wait," he called after her, and she paused, flipping the thick braid over her shoulder. Pale eyes considered him.

"Thank you," he said, his voice swallowed by the night.

She nodded. Turned away. Took a few steps.

"They'll be waiting for me at the station."

She stopped again, but did not turn. Instead, she tilted her head back to stare at the emerging stars, as if consulting them about what to do with this sickly boy. Her arm lifted, and Wil saw to his surprise that she wore gloves. He'd been so fixated on the blade that he hadn't noticed. She extended one finger, crooked it in his direction, and then began walking.

Wil hesitated. The tickets would have no value in half an hour. His fingers burrowed into his coat pocket to brush against the crumpled and damp papers. He must have mangled them earlier when he faced down the older boys.

They would wait for him. He had no doubts about that. They'd lurk in some alley just shy of the station and jump him when he passed, delivering a few solid blows to rid themselves of whatever embarrassing stain their encounter with the woman had left. It was the Harlebone way. The way of all such schools. In twenty years, they'd be drinking wine and smoking cigars in the halls of power, reminiscing about their golden years at Harlebone, proud of the scars and pain they'd endured, even if they'd been the ones to inflict it on each other while the masters looked the other way.

Wil shuddered and hurried after the Rivane woman who was not Rivane.

She was twenty paces ahead of him now and hadn't looked back. He hugged his suitcase to his chest and tried to make his footfalls on the cobbles as soft as possible. Not because he was trying to sneak up on her, but because he didn't want to be too loud. Nor did he want to be noticed. He just wanted to be left alone.

Like always.

So why was he following her?

The woman slowed near a boat painted a luminous silver-gray. It was an odd color for a Rivane boat. Most were shades of blue and green, sometimes red. The color reminded Wil of the dirigibles he'd once seen drifting over Lachfahree when he was much younger. Dirigibles weren't so common these days, their slow elegance eclipsed by the noise and power of the aeroplanes Ben had fallen in love with.

That killed him.

Wil's legs stopped moving, feet glued to the cobbles, the night air raw in his throat. His damaged nose had closed up, and little sparks of pain lanced across his cheeks, but memories of Ben swept aside any worries about the bleeding starting afresh. They surged up like floodwaters, threatening to drown him. Gray fingers encroached on the edges of his vision, narrowing to a tunnel through which he watched the woman leap the gap between bank and boat. She landed and looked back at him.

Someone or something was singing, and Wil couldn't tell where the song came from. It keened in sympathy with his loss.

Wil's vision blurred, tears stinging his eyes. Something bumped and brushed against his leg, and Wil dashed away the tears, staring down into the amber eyes of a gray cat. They studied each other for a long moment. Then the cat's tail twitched, and it darted away, following the woman aboard the luminous boat.

Wetness trickled from his nose. Snot or blood? Probably both.

The feeling returned to Wil's legs in a stinging rush. He took one step closer to the canal, then another. Pale eyes watched him from above the expensive scarf. A gloved hand stretched out toward him, and Wil reached out to grasp it.

8

And Now It Was Morning

The strange woman hadn't exactly invited him to stay. She'd offered her hand to help him aboard the silver-gray boat, but she'd never given her name or even an explanation for why she'd helped him with the Harlebone boys. If anything, Wil thought she might want him to leave.

Within moments of stepping on the boat, that wasn't an option. His eyelids had succumbed to a terrible gravity, while an elusive song ensnared his thoughts. He hoped it was real, but the melody remained beyond the volume or clarity required to make sense of it. It wasn't a familiar tune, but nor was it unfamiliar. Wil had swayed where he stood, and, after a moment of observation with fists planted on hips, the woman had ushered him down a stairwell and pointed to a piece of furniture trapped somewhere between sofa and cot.

"The train station will still be there tomorrow, I suppose, and you're not struggling for cash," she'd said, eyes lingering on his expensive shoes and suitcase. Then she'd tossed him a quilt and vanished deeper into the boat.

And now it was morning—late morning by the angle of the

light coming through the galley window. Boots clomped about on the aft deck, so she must be awake.

Wil sniffed. No cooking smells. Did that mean he hadn't missed breakfast? He sat up, fingers twisting through the gaps in the quilt he'd slept under last night. It wasn't the finest example of knitting, and he frowned at the uncertain patterns creeping across it. Was this the odd woman's work? More likely that of a grandchild by the inexpert nature of it.

Wil sighed and pushed the meager covering aside. He'd slept in his clothes and tried his best to smooth them out. A quick look around revealed nothing resembling a clock. No matter. He'd studied the train timetables. There would be three departures for the capital today, though only the earliest was an express. That said, he'd lost the exchange value of his tickets for last night, so the cheaper, slower trains were his best bet to stretch what funds he had.

His fingers twitched.

There was some emergency cash hidden in the lining of his suit-case. Or there had been. He'd slept the sleep of the dead. The woman could have ransacked his suitcase while he slept. Could he trust her? Despite her coloring and accent, this was a Rivane boat, and the Rivane had a reputation…

Stop, Wil ordered himself, derailing that train of thought.

A train of thought his mother would have boarded eagerly.

Or his brother Hal.

Wil had never met one of the canal folk. In fact, his only experience of the Rivane was this woman, who looked and sounded just like him, driving off a pack of bullies before offering him a place to sleep. Of course, she had threatened those boys with a knife, so the encounter hadn't left an entirely positive impression.

Wil massaged his temples as they throbbed. A familiar, dull band of pressure squeezed his skull, and he forced himself to draw a few shallow, ragged breaths.

"You're awake then."

Wil looked up, startled. How had he missed her boots clomping down the steps to the galley? He stood, ducking for fear of bashing his head against the low ceiling of the cabin.

"Yes, um. Thank you?"

The woman shrugged and pulled at her braid. With the benefit of the morning light, he could see that her hair was orange, laced with strands of white. She'd also removed her scarf, revealing a face that looked younger than the white woven through her braid would suggest, though her skin was an unfashionable tan, and somewhat weathered to boot.

Her pale eyes ran the length of him, and Wil felt naked beneath their appraisal. He fought down the urge to cover himself with his hands despite being fully dressed.

"Washroom is on the left." She pointed toward a narrow corridor that led deeper into the boat. "I'll put a kettle on so we can get something warm in you before you head to the station. Those boys are long gone back north."

Wil started to thank her, but she'd already turned away, making a deafening racket as she rummaged through the galley's cabinets. Then his bladder reminded him of how long he'd slept, and Wil hurried for the washroom.

9

Lest the Whispers and Shadows Find You

The tea had an odd, spicy aftertaste that Wil couldn't decide if he liked or not, and he wasn't sure if it was helping the throbbing that plagued his head. The woman sat opposite him at the small galley table, plucking hazelnuts from the bowl of assorted nuts and dried fruit they were sharing for breakfast. Should he ask her name? A dozen times the words threatened to leap from his tongue, but he always swallowed them. Instead, he referred to her as "the captain" in the privacy of his own thoughts.

The captain's fingers dipped into the bowl and fished out another hazelnut. She glanced up at the distant, mournful shriek of a train whistle. "That'll be the express leaving," she said, her eyes boring into his. Left unsaid was the question of when Wil himself would be leaving. She wasn't suggesting he do so immediately, but she gave every sign that she intended to leave soon.

When? And where was she going?

Why should he care?

Wil needed to get his things together and head for the train station. The winter break was eight weeks long, but if he didn't turn up at the family estates in the next few days, his family would ask questions and might send someone to the school looking for him.

He needed to move and keep moving if he was going to track down Ben's Callie in the Smoke and…

And what?

What was he hoping would come of any meeting with her? He hadn't planned that far ahead, always assuming he'd fall at the first hurdle and end up retreating to the north. Did he hope Callie had some last message from Ben, that she could provide him with some way to ease the pain of his brother's sudden passing? Was he hoping the noise and bustle of the city would occupy his mind and leave no empty spaces and silences to fill?

Wil looked away from the captain, his eyes roving the boat's narrow cabin. Tacked to the opposite wall was a map marked with red lines and green, spidery notes scrawled in blank ink in the gaps between the lines.

"Where are you headed next?" he asked.

"Why?"

He glanced back and saw that her own gaze had shifted to the map.

"Just making conversation."

"Indeed."

Something bumped Wil's leg, and he tilted his head to peek under the table at a gray cat. It looked a shade darker than last night. Maybe it wasn't the same cat? Wil snuck fingers off the table and scratched behind the cat's ears.

"So?" he asked.

The captain tugged at her braid and sighed. Wil watched her jaw tense and then relax, almost like she was having some silent struggle with herself. Or a conversation. The cat licked Wil's finger with a rough tongue, and the captain frowned. At long last, she nodded and stood.

"You can store your suitcase under the cot," she said.

"What?"

The captain pulled gloves from her belt and dragged them over her fingers. "I expect you to work for your passage."

"I'm sorry, but—"

"You have any other shoes? Ones that can take some wear?"

Wil's head reeled. He hadn't noticed her looking at his shoes—shoes his mother had bought for him—but now they felt ridiculous.

"I don't know—"

Her chin darted to the corridor at the rear of the cabin, though her eyes steered carefully clear of his. "There are some extras in the closet opposite the washroom. Find a pair near your size and change into something you don't mind getting grimy. Meet me up top in five minutes."

It was the most words she'd strung together since they'd met, and they tumbled out in a rush, almost like she was nervous. About what? Wil stood dumbstruck, watching her stride through the galley and out the door, clomping up the steps to the deck.

Boots. Heavy boots.

Right.

He only caught himself as he dragged open the closet door and stared at the mess inside. There were boots, sandals, coats, coils of rope, a few tools he couldn't place. Why did she have extras?

"Stop it, Wil," he muttered. "What are you doing?"

But he'd already spotted his new footwear. He crouched and pulled a pair of cracked gray boots from the mess at the bottom of the closet. As he did, the band of pressure on his head loosened its hold a touch, and the singing he'd heard last night tickled his ears.

Only it wasn't in his ears.

It was inside his head.

A sudden scratching knocked Wil out of his reverie, and he twisted to see the cat stretching and yawning in a patch of sunlight, claws dragging across floorboards.

"Move and keep moving," he breathed. "Lest the whispers and shadows find you."

The cat blinked at him and seemed to shrug. Then it curled up in its patch of sun, tail wrapping around its body, not caring that a stranger much bigger than itself stood just a few feet away, a stranger that could accidentally step on it or purposefully cause it harm. How did it know he wouldn't?

Wil pulled off his shoes and slid his toes into the ugly boots, wondering if he would have actually exchanged the train tickets.

Now that the train was no longer in the picture, he made an honest assessment. Would he have exchanged them, or would he have panicked when he got to the ticket window, realizing he didn't know anybody in the Smoke, that he didn't know where or how to find Callie? Would he have just swallowed his half-baked plan and gone back north to his family estates?

He would have, wouldn't he?

If he was honest, he knew that. So what now?

He looked at the cat, looked around the cabin.

This was another kind of escape, but was it a better one? How would a canal make him forget what had happened to Ben?

The eight weeks of break stretched before Wil, almost infinite in prospect, though he wasn't sure whether that prospect was hopeful or terrifying.

10

A Faint Blush of Light
Painted the Glass

"Damn her," Wil muttered.

He stumbled down the steps and through the cabin door, breathing hard from his aborted pursuit of the Rivane girl, every inch of him aching or blistered or bleeding from days of unaccustomed labor. How many days was it now? Three? Five? Had it been a week already?

All day he'd been mired in scraping the hull and coiling mooring lines, and then the captain had insisted that he needed to fetch more water for the boat's tanks before the sun set. He'd returned, carrying two full pails, to find a small Rivane girl darting up out of the cabin. Wil had shouted at her and tried to give chase, but the girl had vanished into the twilit evening like a spooked rabbit.

He'd trudged back to the boat along the towpath, hugging himself as the cold of the oncoming evening set in, chilling his sweat, setting his entire body to shivering. Down the steps on numb feet, the muscles in his legs gone to jelly. He banged his hip against the galley counter and didn't notice until the pain fought its way past all the other aches that plagued him.

Going to bruise nicely, that one.

And it wouldn't be alone.

Arms. Legs. Even the nose he'd damaged before he'd started working on the boat. Red-purple wings spread across his cheeks, fading to yellow and green around the edges of the bruises.

Wil choked down bile. He'd only caught glimpses of the state of his face reflected in the canal, but that had been enough. Every morning brought a fresh crust of dried blood on his nostrils and upper lip. The masters had merely made sure they stopped the bleeding on his last night at Harlebone, convinced he would be home soon enough. Any further medical needs could be handled by his family. A weak part of him wished he was home for the winter break, waiting for a doctor to be summoned to the estate to ensure he wasn't dying.

Wil's steps dragged as he made his way to the cot. He'd need to go back outside and put the water he'd fetched in the tank, but he needed to check his suitcase first, and he was dreading doing it. There was no sign of the captain on the boat and no note to say where she'd gone or when she'd return. The shivering intensified, and Wil buried his trembling hands in his armpits, seeking warmth.

The girl had been in the cabin.

Unattended.

With his suitcase.

And his money.

Wil sank to his knees and reached under the cot with fingers shaking like an invalid's. The case didn't seem to be disturbed, but what if the girl was a thief? The Rivane had a reputation, after all.

He paused, a warm flush climbing his cheeks and pushing back the chill.

Those were his parents' prejudices, prejudices he hated. But they were hard to ignore.

He popped the catches and flung open the case, trembling fingers examining the secret spot under the lining.

His breath escaped in a rush.

The money was still there.

Because the girl hadn't found it or because she wasn't a thief?

"Stop it, Wil." He twisted around, pressing his back against the uncomfortable angles of the cot, one hand on his suitcase.

And blinked.

In a small green vase on the narrow galley dining table stood a bunch of yellow and blue flowers, tied with a yellow ribbon. It hadn't been there when he'd choked down a crust of bread and some dried fruit for lunch, and he couldn't imagine the captain taking the time to arrange flowers.

The Rivane girl? Was that why she'd been in the cabin? And how had she found flowers in midwinter?

As Wil's heart slowed, a sound filled his ears above the hammering of blood in his ears. Something that wasn't quite music flowed into his mind, settling like the still waters of the canal, waters he'd watched all yesterday as the captain piloted the silver boat farther and farther away from the glowering brick pile of Harlebone School. The black and gray of his childhood gave way to green fields and blue sky, all mirrored in the placid line of water that cut through the countryside of Saxe-Colraine like a blade.

Flowers filled his vision, yellow and blue over green.

Why had the girl…?

He yawned, wincing as sharp pains sparked from his nose across his cheeks. His head dipped once. Twice…

Wil shook himself awake in freezing darkness. How long had he been asleep? Where was the captain? Groping blindly, he dragged a blanket around his shoulders, then stood to make his way to the darkened galley. There was a lantern on the steps outside, and he found it by starlight, fumbling with the cold metal. How to light the thing? He didn't have any matches, didn't know where the captain would keep anything of the sort. So how…?

His finger brushed something at the bottom of the lantern, and a faint blush of light painted the glass.

What?

He moved his finger and found the thing he'd touched—a notched wheel at the base of the lantern. He pressed his finger down, moved the wheel, and was rewarded with a brighter glow, tinted blue.

Wil blinked at the light and frowned. He was too tired to

contemplate this discovery now. He needed sleep, needed the captain here to answer his questions. Where was she? She should—

Wil froze. The water. He'd left the pails outside and then fallen asleep. Irresponsible idiot. What would she say if she tripped over them in the dark?

Taking the steps two at a time, he reached the aft deck and held the lantern aloft. The two pails lay where he'd abandoned them on the towpath, and a cat paused in drinking from one to turn flashing eyes on Wil.

"Damn it all."

He hung the lantern on a hook jutting from the hull and then crossed the plank to shore. Sheets of ice floated on the water, and he fished them out with numb fingers, tossing them into the canal as he brought the pails back to the boat and filled the tanks. Job done, he stowed the pails in a locker and glanced up and down the towpath. Still no sign of the captain.

Wil snatched the lantern off the hook and made his way back down to the galley, spinning the wheel at the lantern's base until the blue-white glow filled the interior of the cabin. He set the lantern down on the counter. Better get changed into nightclothes and stow the case. Then he could put the lantern back outside for the captain.

If she returned.

"Stop it," he growled, half expecting a response.

Nothing. Only silence and empty shadows. He almost laughed at himself.

Almost.

Kneeling, nose throbbing as the blood rushed to his head, Wil pushed the suitcase back under the cot. A flash of yellow beneath the cot stopped him. Eyes in the darkness. Wil blinked and held his breath. Maybe the shadows weren't so empty? Then the eyes moved and a yawning gray cat emerged from beneath the cot.

"So that's where you've been hiding yourself. You had a friend visiting outside," he said, then paused. Had it been a different cat outside? He'd seen what he thought was the same gray cat several times that day, but now he wasn't sure if it was just one cat or a series of gray cats in different shades.

The cat stretched and sighed, then slinked past Wil, one flank brushing Wil's leg. He didn't turn to watch it go. His gaze fixed on what the cat had been sitting on, a vague rectangular shape in the shadows. He reached under the cot and pulled out a book. The cover was dark leather, worn and caked with a layer of dust. No markings of any kind. He thumbed the book open and stared at the dense scrawl of ink decorating the pages, a blend of drawings and writing in an inexpert hand. The drawings were childish and most of the words misspelled, though they were close enough for him to grasp their meaning. At least some of them. Not every word was in Saxer script.

Was it a diary of some sort, the captain's perhaps? But surely someone who spoke like her could spell?

Boots on the steps.

Wil shoved the book into his suitcase and snapped the latches. By the time the captain entered the cabin, he had already stowed the case beneath the cot.

11

The Bird Dream

Within the dream, all of Wil's thoughts were bent on escape.

Escape from the boats and the canals.

Escape from his children and husband.

Children? Husband?

He didn't have any children, and he certainly didn't have a husband.

The objection evaporated and gave way to thoughts of water, bugs, drudgery, and skirts.

Skirts?

The only rival for his obsession with escape was fear. Fear of the next time her husband's drinking unleashed the beast.

Her husband?

Wil felt his sense of self slipping away, becoming a passenger in his own mind. Only he wasn't in his own mind, was he? He was riding in someone else's, someone with a husband and children. A husband named Remmi.

Her Remmi was a beautiful man with skin the muddy brown of silt stirred up by a narrowboat's passage and eyes the pale green of leaf buds about to burst open. His lashes were longer and darker than her own.

Was it him she loved or the idea of him? He was beautiful, yes, but beautiful like an object of art or a stunning landscape. That wasn't love, was it?

Her Remmi thought himself fated for more than a life of canals and locks, deliveries and simple labor. In every village, at every mooring, he sought more. More money. More respect. Something more. Anything more.

But being a Rivane man in Saxe-Colraine, everything conspired against him. The color of his skin. His accent. His lack of schooling. Canal folk were already at the bottom of the social ladder. Frustration with his life led to inevitable anger, and when Remmi's anger boiled over, it scalded his children.

And his wife.

She hunched over the washing, cursing the heavy skirts of her people and the mass of dark hair that tradition would not let her cut. Hunger gnawed at her. Remmi had taken the last of the brown bread and cheese and gone seeking work at the farmstead bordering their mooring. More coin in their coffers would be nice, but she feared what he would do with any money he earned. There was a town a mile or so back down the canal. Towns meant pubs. Pubs meant beer and spirits. Beer and spirits would inevitably lead to shouting and blood and bruises.

She straightened and pushed balled fists into the small of her back, thankful that her boys were off amusing themselves somewhere and not pestering her with their noise and need for attention and the constant violence they inflicted on each other. Would they grow up any different from their father?

Movement in the sky caught her eye, and she whipped up one bronzed hand to shade her eyes.

There. A bird, gliding. Big one. A hawk, maybe?

The bird's wings spread against a backdrop of pale blue sky and wispy white clouds. She envied the creature its freedom. The boat was a prison. These canals were a prison. Motherhood and marriage and tradition. So many prisons.

But the bird was free.

What she wouldn't give to be that bird.

12

A Strange Sigil

Wil pulled the brush back from beneath the cot, dragging out enough cat hair that he could have fashioned a small rat from it. His nose tickled, but he fought the sneeze, worried what might come out of his almost healed nose. He dumped the hair in the bin beside him and straightened, pressing a fist to his back and stretching. With this much hair in the cabin, there had to be multiple cats. Still, the hair was always gray, and he'd only ever seen one cat at a time.

Grinding the fist deeper, he tried to work out the knot in his back, aware that part of the pain was an echo from the woman he'd been dreaming about.

That he was dreaming of being.

Setting the brush back on the floorboards, he returned to cleaning, letting his mind drift back over his recent dreams. Had his few stolen glances at the diary he'd found inspired them? Possibly. It was hard to parse the writing, much less make out any semblance of a narrative. Cramped sketches and observations of only a sentence or three filled the pages, though the author didn't observe such niceties as punctuation and proper grammar. At least in the Saxer language. Wil wasn't sure about the other scripts and languages. Did the

Rivane have their own language? They must. Why had he never wondered about it before?

The dreams, on the other hand, were pure narrative, and he could remember them better than any dream prior to his life on the boat. In fact, they were the only dreams he'd had since he'd come aboard *Cloud Dancer*. No name adorned the boat's hull, and Wil had only learned of its existence when a passing boat called out, "Hoy, the *Cloud Dancer*," to get the captain's attention. They hadn't used the captain's name, and she still hadn't given it to him, though she trusted him enough to leave him alone with the boat when she vanished off into various towns and villages for hours at a time.

Three weeks he'd been on the boat, and the captain had paid a dozen mysterious visits in that time. What was she doing?

Wil dumped another load of dust, debris, and cat hair in the bin and pushed to his feet. *Cloud Dancer* didn't seem to carry any cargo, and the captain wasn't making any sales that Wil was aware of. They also didn't seem to need fuel. He fetched water every morning, but he'd seen no stockpiles of wood or coal. So what were they burning in the stove that heated the boat and cooked their food? What, in point of fact, was powering *Cloud Dancer's* engine?

Wil frowned, thinking of the strange lantern that didn't burn oil, then allowed himself a bitter smile. "Rivane magic," he intoned, waving his fingers as he made his way toward the galley. As he passed the map tacked to the wall, he tried, as always, to figure out where they were. The writing was symbolic and representative of no language he was familiar with. Presumably it was some sort of Rivane code.

His finger traced the canal the captain had identified for him, though she hadn't explained where they were on that canal or where Saint Malvern's Green was located. Three weeks since they'd left that town, more than a third of his break, and Wil only knew that they were chugging along a westerly route bending a shade north. Unfortunately, the map focused on the canals and represented them as straight lines, so there were no bends in the canal or borders between land and sea that might have proved helpful in narrowing down their location. Nor were there any markings for topographical features. He tapped the map at his best guess at their location, eyes trailing up and left to a strange sigil drawn across the line of the canal.

What could that be?

"Your first lock tomorrow. Leaving the flatlands."

Wil spun around. For all the noise her boots made on the deck and the steps, the captain could move in silence when she wanted. Wil suspected she only trod heavily when she wanted to express displeasure or annoyance. He would need to remember that when he stole moments to examine the diary or check the hidden stash of money in the suitcase.

The captain's eyes dropped to the bin. "Put the rubbish out. We need to make six miles by nightfall."

Voices Drifted Through the Mist Like Phantoms

The next morning might have dawned on a different world. Fog pulled a thick blanket around *Cloud Dancer*, leaving only a narrow band of canal visible. Frost coated the vegetation drifting past on either bank, and thin scabs of ice covered much of the canal. For the first hour of their journey, they endured a grating symphony of grinding and cracking as *Cloud Dancer* pushed through the ice.

During that hour, dawn progressed to early morning. Though the pale disk of the sun struggled to penetrate the mist, it must have brought enough warmth to thaw the ice. Now the only sound was the occasional crunch from a stubborn patch of ice and the muted grumble of *Cloud Dancer's* engine, though the thick fog muffled even those infrequent sounds.

Wil pushed back damp hair in need of a trim and peered ahead. The fog was playing tricks with time, and it wouldn't have surprised him to hear that they'd been drifting through it for three hours, maybe even five.

"Lock's ahead," the captain called from the stern.

Wil frowned. How could she tell? From his position perched at the prow of the boat, he couldn't see much beyond a dozen feet. He wasn't even sure how the captain was navigating.

"More Rivane magic," he murmured, trusting the fog to swallow his words.

The pitch of the engine changed, and Wil felt the boat slow beneath him. The captain's instructions over a hurried breakfast of stale bread and hard cheese had been minimal. When she nosed into the bank, he'd disembark and tie a loose mooring, then wait for the lock keeper to come and collect him. On a less miserable day, she'd said, he could have made his own way up to the lock. Today, he would need a guide. When the keeper came down to fetch him, he was to follow orders and assist as necessary.

How was Wil supposed to know what was necessary? How was he supposed to even see the lock, much less its keeper? He could express these doubts in his own mind, but when they threatened to trouble his tongue, he bit down on them, convinced he would embarrass himself.

The outline of the bank grew more solid as they drifted toward it, and again the engine's growl shifted pitch as the captain engaged the bow thrusters. *Cloud Dancer's* horn lanced the mist, and Wil clapped hands over his ears too late to deaden the sound. Half-deafened, he snatched up the coiled bow line and leapt to the bank. He dragged the boat against the side of the canal and looped the rope around a wooden mooring post, tying a loose knot. He waved back to the captain, unsure if she could see him. Her own form was ghostly but backlit by the brighter eastern sky. She sounded the horn again.

They waited.

And waited some more.

Wil turned to squint up the towpath toward where the lock must be.

"Must not be up there yet."

Wil jumped at the captain's voice right beside him, but she didn't seem to notice. Or maybe she was sparing his blushes?

"You'll have to fetch him."

"Me?"

She glanced at him out of the corner of her eye. "You're working for your passage, aren't you?"

Wil swallowed the excuses welling up about how he didn't know the lock keeper, how this was his first lock, how he wasn't comfortable with new people.

"Where is he?"

"Follow the towpath, and you'll come to two sets of stairs. The ones along the canal lead to the lock. The ones heading inland will bring you to an inn." Her mouth twisted into an expression that wasn't quite a smile. "That's where he'll be. Ask for Old Garfo."

"Old Garfo?"

A Rivane name. Why should that surprise him? If most canal boats were Rivane, why wouldn't the Rivane also work the locks? Why had he never considered that before? Was it because he'd always assumed all Rivane spent their lives aboard boats? Who said the lock keeper didn't? Maybe Old Garfo lived on a boat moored around here.

"Go," the captain ordered. She strode back into the mist.

Wil nodded, though she wasn't looking at him any longer, and started making his way along the towpath. His ears strained to make out footsteps, animal sounds, anything that might indicate he wasn't the only living thing about. Two stone staircases loomed out of the mist. Treacherous looking. Wet, maybe icy. Wil flinched as something blurred past him, then tried to laugh as he saw it was the gray cat. Or one of them, anyway. It sped up the steps to the lock, and Wil shook his head, flinging droplets from his sodden hair. He inched his way up the steps in pursuit, wishing there was a handrail.

The path at the top of the steps was gravel and crunched beneath his boots. Ahead, he could make out the dim shape of a building, its windows aglow. Voices drifted through the mist like phantoms, unattached to physical forms, a chorus of ghosts. The smoke from the chimney settled in the still air, thickening the fog.

Wil paused on the doorstep, one palm pressed flat against the door, ready to push it inward, when the wood vanished from beneath his hand, yanked away with sudden violence, and Wil staggered forward.

14

Old Garfo

The heat and noise smacked Wil like a wall. A trio of bearded men barged him aside as they left the inn, slamming the door behind them. He tried to make himself as small as possible, but a barmaid had already planted herself in front of him, hands on hips, a towel draped over her shoulder.

"Bit late for breakfast, love, but I can put something together for you from what's left."

Wil shook his head, lost for words, pain pulsing behind his left eye. The onslaught was too loud, too fragrant, too riotous.

"You sick or something?" The barmaid's eyes narrowed.

"Garfo," Wil managed at last. "Looking for Old Garfo."

She glanced down at his garb—mismatched odds and ends from his suitcase and the captain's closet of castoffs. "You Rivane?"

Wil stared at her, not knowing how to answer—was he or wasn't he?—but the barmaid only shrugged.

"Don't much look or sound the part, but..." she twisted to shout over her shoulder. "Garf! Customer." She quirked an eyebrow at Wil. "Something to eat?"

Wil shook his head, and the barmaid vanished, leaving him

standing in the middle of the room, turning awkwardly, aware of the eyes on him, none of them Rivane that he could tell. Mostly farmers and tradesmen, and few friendly faces among them.

A hand landed on his shoulder and spun him around. A face framed by stiff whiskers the color of iron leaned in close, one eye milky, the other spearing right through him. "What boat?"

"*Cloud Dancer.*"

"So she's picking up strays now? Never figured her for the type." The bearded man spat on the floor and turned away. "Better not keep her waiting at the lock. Got a temper, that one."

This was Old Garfo the lock keeper?

The old man thunked away, but Wil's boots were stuck to the floor. Old Garfo's left leg ended just below the knee. The rest had been replaced by a metal rod ending in a ball where his foot should be.

Old Garfo yanked the door open and glanced over his shoulder. "Come on then, stray."

The noise, heat, and smells almost shoved Wil out of the inn, trailed by half-hearted curses about the Rivane, and he hurried to catch up to the lock keeper, whose awkward, swinging gait was deceptively fast.

"You ever work a lock before?" Old Garfo asked when Wil caught up to him, not sparing him a glance. The fog had thinned a bit, but visibility was still poor.

"N-no," Wil stammered.

Old Garfo grunted and growled something under his breath about untrained boys.

The pale sun was doing its best to burn off the mist. By the time they reached the lock, taking a different path than the one Wil had taken up, the full length of the lock was visible. Half again as long as *Cloud Dancer*, it was wide enough to accommodate two canal boats side by side. Massive wooden gates bound each end, holding in water flecked with bits of ice.

Old Garfo's swinging stride took him to the downhill gate closest to *Cloud Dancer*, where he crouched next to a squat metal pillar. Wil peered over his shoulder as the bearded man whispered something song-like, fingers dancing over gears and levers. The earth rumbled and shifted beneath them, and Wil gasped. Old Garfo pushed upright again and fixed Wil with his one good eye. He hooked a finger at the gate.

"See them beams?"

Wil shook his head. "I'm sorry…" The rumbling beneath them was louder, and water gushed and splashed somewhere nearby.

Old Garfo sighed. "The big wooden bits attached to the gate."

Wil glanced at the gate and nodded.

The lock keeper pointed to the far side. "You go over there and push that beam when I tell you."

Wil nodded again, then frowned, glancing up and down the lock. "How do I get over there?"

This time, Old Garfo grinned, but there was little kindness in it. "Gotta cross the gate, boy." He lifted his ruined leg and waved the metal rod around. "My clambering days are over."

Wil swallowed and tried not to shiver. The small ledge bolted to the outside of the gate was just about wide enough to cross. He eyed the drop to the canal, then glanced at the lock side of the gate. The water in the lock was sinking, wisps of steam skating along the surface. What…?

"Go on."

Just a few weeks ago, Wil would have refused, would not even have considered crossing the narrow gate. But now? Now he was a few steps onto the walkway before the fear enveloped him, sending chills radiating from spine to fingers and toes. His head throbbed, but he focused on putting one numb foot in front of the other. Just a few more steps.

There was definitely steam rising from the sinking water in the lock. How was that possible? Warmth bathed his outthrust right arm, while the left was almost frozen. It hung over a drop into icy water. Logically, Wil knew it wasn't as far down as it looked, but still—

His ill-fitting boot slipped off the damp wood, leaving his foot dangling over the drop.

Wil swayed.

And caught his balance on one leg.

Then staggered the final few steps across.

He spun around with a triumphant smile just in time to see Old Garfo wiping a look of horror from his face.

15

Speaking of the Devil

The look vanished almost before Wil could process it, replaced by a scowl. Old Garfo waved him toward the beam and took his own position on the far side of the gate. Once again, he bent down, this time above a metal box bolted to the beam, whispering while his fingers danced. A shifting, grinding noise sounded beneath them, and water gushed from the bottom of the gate, emptying the lock even more rapidly, plumes of steam rising where the lock water splashed down into the canal.

Wil put his back against the wooden beam, mirroring Old Garfo on the far side of the lock. Below them, the sound of rushing water slowed. Something Old Garfo had done with the post and then the box on the beam had caused the lock to drain while heating the remaining water.

But how? There hadn't seemed to be any mechanical effort on Old Garfo's part, and they certainly weren't burning any fuel to power a machine or a boiler of any kind. Was the lock like *Cloud Dancer's* mysterious engine?

Speaking of the devil...

The luminous silver-gray hull emerged from the mists below them, the captain a wraith at the stern, her wide-brimmed hat twitching back as she glanced up at them. Wil suppressed the childish urge to wave at her.

"Put your back into it, stray."

Wil hadn't realized the water had slowed to a trickle until he heard Old Garfo's shout. He looked over at the lock keeper leaning back against his beam, boots wedged against stones set in the paving. Wil placed his boots against the first stone on his side of the gate and pushed. One step. Two. Another stone appeared beneath his feet and he braced his foot against it, pushed again.

Clever.

But why use some hidden Rivane magic to drain the locks and power boats but not to open these gates? Maybe the workings of engines weren't obvious to a casual, outside observer? Maybe the manual opening of the gates was a disguise of sorts?

Below, a last rush of trapped water flooded out from the lock, and he saw the captain twitch the tiller to keep *Cloud Dancer's* bow pointed at the open gate.

Wil's beam stopped moving with a sudden jolt that slammed the heavy wood into his back. He bit back a cry and stood, pressing fingers to the raw flesh, knowing there would be bruises tomorrow. Below, *Cloud Dancer's* engine throbbed as the captain steered her through the gate. Movement further back along the canal caught Wil's eye, and he squinted at another boat emerging from the mist, this one dark green and shorter than *Cloud Dancer*. The man at the tiller was tall for a Rivane, white hair pulled back in a ponytail.

"Quit gawking, stray. There's still work to do."

Old Garfo was already halfway back up the lock, walking with his curious, swing-legged gait. How had he lost the bottom half of his leg? Wil longed to ask but knew he didn't have the courage. Maybe the captain would know, but he was almost as afraid of asking her as he was of asking Old Garfo. He jogged in pursuit on his side of the lock.

"She'll toss you a line. Pull her tight to the side."

Wil nodded even though the lock keeper was busy watching the green boat maneuver into the lock beside *Cloud Dancer*. Wil shifted his gaze to the new boat, then had to duck when a coil of rope came sailing up from the lock. He swallowed an oath and bent to grab the line, pulling *Cloud Dancer* against the wall of the lock. Old Garfo did the same on the other side, twisting the green boat's line around a post with practiced efficiency. Wil copied him, then turned to find Old Garfo already back at his beam, pushing his half of the down-hill gate closed. Wil jogged back to close his half of the gate, sweat beading his brow despite the chill of the morning.

As the gate swung closed with a shiver, he heard something oddly like a child's voice. An animal, perhaps? Wil cocked an ear, trying to listen for it, but Old Garfo was shouting at him again. He looked up to see the lock keeper halfway along the lock again, motioning him to follow, but the lock keeper's eyes looked strange. Shining. Was he crying?

Wil hurried back along the lock, copying the lock keeper as the old man swooped to snatch up a second line tossed from the green boat. Wil watched him kneel beside a post near the far gate, identical to the one he'd manipulated before. Again, the earth rumbled. Water gushed from holes in the lock.

"Hold her!" Old Garfo shouted, even as Wil felt the rope in his hand go taut.

In Wil's head, a younger man's shout echoed the old man's.

Followed by a child's scream.

16

Twenty Months Ago in a Lachfahree Barn

Wil lay on his back, hands laced behind his head, staring at the patch of blue sky framed by the hole in the barn's roof. Rough straw pricked his back and dust tickled his nose, but he relished these discomforts. Better than remaining at the manor house. No matter how many rooms it boasted, no matter what comforts of wealth and status it provided, it was still his father's house, haunted by his father's shouts.

And screams and threats and weeping.

Wil's fingers tightened, tugging at his dark hair, prompting tears. At least that was honest pain. Real pain. Not what his father suffered. Screaming at ghosts. Staring at visions no one else could see.

Why did his mother persist in keeping him here? For years, his father had only had the occasional bad day, and that wasn't difficult to endure. She could usually calm him with laudanum, get him to bed, and in the morning he would wake as if nothing strange had happened.

But lately…

Something rustled in the rafters of the barn, and Wil's eyes twitched toward the sound, hunting for movement. A bird, perhaps?

The patch of blue sky called to him with its promise of soothing escape, but Wil had to know what the noise was. He frowned and sat up, peering into the gloom.

"Hello?" he called, not expecting an answer but hoping it would stir whatever creature was hiding there into motion.

Sighing, he stretched his arms over his head, feeling the ache where the bruise would form tomorrow, the broad welt on his back where his father's cane had lashed him. Had the old man even realized that his blow had landed? Had he seen Wil's face and known it was his son he struck in his incoherent wrath? It was difficult to tell when the old man spent more than half his days in a kind of waking dream, conversing with phantoms and raging against unseen foes.

Old man?

His father, Raymonthe Cathermay-Gravence, the seventh lord Breymerick, was just a few years past forty. And yet the last few months had aged him such that one might mistake him for being well into his sixth decade. The fair hair, almost white like Wil's eldest brother Hal's, was falling out in clumps, and his skin had faded to a dry, grayish pallor. Though Wil's mother did what she could to keep up appearances, several of the servants had already fled, including his father's valet. Wil had seen the bruise on the man's cheek and the blood trickling from his lip the night before he vanished.

Who could Wil appeal to for help? His mother wouldn't hear any words against her husband. She was too afraid word would get out, that disgrace would follow, even if Wil suspected she would relish the role of tragic heroine wedded to a lunatic. The lurid drama of it would appeal to a woman who consumed novels and gossip more than food.

And his brothers?

Hal was working down in the capital, learning to manipulate the financial machinery of the family empire to ensure their continued influence and wealth. He would be even more keen to keep the family's reputation intact than their mother would be.

And Ben?

Ben would come if he knew how bad things were, but he was at Harlebone. The masters would read any mail intended for the students, and Wil couldn't risk word of his father's madness reaching the school. The family could not bear the ignominy.

Again a noise drifted down from the rafters, but Wil's eyes, adjusted now to the murk, picked out movement. Too big to be a bird. A cat, perhaps?

Still too big. More like…

A child?

An image swam in his mind. A little girl swinging from the rafters at the end of a rope. She wasn't playing. Not when the rope twisted round her neck and her head lolled at such an obscene angle.

What was—?

A scream filled Wil's ears, and it wasn't until his throat grew raw that he realized he was the one screaming.

17

Shapes Moved in the Steamy Mist

The sound of rushing water filled Wil's ears, drowning out the screaming, and he blinked back to the present, letting the memory of the barn and the spectral child evaporate, leaving him cold and shivering. Two boats rose toward him through a haze of steam. The roar of the filling lock was immense, but the noise played tricks on Wil's ears. Suggestions of shouts and screams blended with the water's song. Shapes moved in the steamy mist. Were they real? He did not dare close his eyes. Nor did he dare drop the mooring rope to cover his ears. Shutting eyes and ears never helped, anyway. In his experience, it only made things worse when his thoughts ran rampant with fewer distractions.

Instead, Wil focused his attention on Old Garfo, leaning back against the rope holding the green boat, eyes fixed on the gate. There was sorrow in his look. And anger. Was it something to do with the screams Wil wished he hadn't heard?

As if feeling Wil's eyes upon him, the lock keeper's gaze flickered up. He nodded, glanced down at the boats, and a veil dropped over his features, masking any emotion lingering there. Wil shifted his attention to the captain. She always wore a similar mask. What was she hiding?

The water filling the lock slowed, and Wil glanced up to see Old Garfo waving him toward the gate. Time to free the boats. Wil found his position, placed his back against the heavy wooden beam, and pushed. It was tougher going this time with the weight of the water to shift, but once Wil got the beam moving, something within the gate itself seemed to assist him, a presence that felt almost alive.

The green boat exited the lock first, the man with the white hair bound at the nape of his neck waving to Old Garfo and nodding his thanks to Wil. The lock keeper watched him go, the mask slipping for a moment to reveal something that might have been pity or sympathy. Then the old man spun around on his metal stump and made his swing-legged way to a small shack Wil hadn't noticed before in the heavy fog. No word of goodbye. No parting glance for *Cloud Dancer*.

"Meet me at the mooring," the captain called as she steered out of the lock.

Wil stared after Old Garfo for a moment, and then at the open gate. Was this how it had begun with his father? Ghosts in gates and engines? How long did he have before his thoughts and emotions began to unravel? He'd never had the courage to ask his mother when she first noticed the signs in his father.

Of course, there was an alternative explanation. He might not be imagining it. Maybe the Rivane possessed some hidden power over machines? But how could that be? Someone would have noticed. Or was it like the railroads or flight—just another marvel that most people accepted because they never bothered with why it worked or the science that had gone into making it work?

Wil shook off his reverie and jogged along the towpath. The captain was already nosing *Cloud Dancer* into the mooring, and she wouldn't be pleased if his dawdling delayed them.

18

Patterns That Were
Becoming Familiar

The green boat was a quarter-mile ahead of them, chugging along the canal at the same pace as *Cloud Dancer*. To their left, an embankment gave way to fields left barren for winter. Broken stalks and mud. An occasional farmhouse sent tendrils of smoke into the gray sky.

Wil glanced up at the green boat from time to time as he practiced his knots, catching snatches of music drifting back on the wind. Some sort of stringed instrument accompanied by a low voice. How was the man both playing and piloting his boat? And why did the song seem to blend with *Cloud Dancer's* soft hum in his ears?

"Loop first," the captain broke into his reverie, and Wil glanced down at his hands. He'd done the knot wrong, but how had she seen? His back was to her, shielding the rope from her view. Could she tell by the way his arms moved?

Sighing, Wil released the knot and stretched his aching fingers, preparing to try again. Better an ache in his fingers than one in his head. It was strange to realize that the aches and pains from his labor aboard the boat had left him healthier than he'd felt in over a year. The monotonous work also kept his mind occupied enough that it didn't throw up as many distractions of sounds and sights and smells that weren't there.

Pity it didn't silence the boat's song.

Wil's mouth opened, and a question about the song almost escaped his lips before he bit down, keeping it caged. He didn't have the courage to ask the captain about it. Was he more afraid she would think him insane or confirm that she heard it too? Which would be worse?

"How long until the next lock?" he asked instead.

"Two days," the captain replied.

If she had a plan for where they were going, Wil wasn't aware of it. She hardly spared a glance for the map in the galley, and they weren't carrying cargo unless she'd hidden it in her cabin. He'd been over every other inch of the boat while cleaning or doing maintenance work, but he was reluctant to invade her private space. Still, whenever she left the boat to visit towns or villages near their moorings, she didn't seem to take much with her besides a satchel. Was there more or less in it when she returned? Wil wasn't sure.

"Are they all like Old Garfo's?" he asked. Lock keepers whispering to magic posts, he meant. Haunted by a girl's screams, he meant.

"They are like our boats," she replied.

That wasn't an answer.

Or was it?

"How?"

"Same function, but they all feel different."

Wil's fingers moved in patterns that were becoming familiar, twisting and tugging at the knots, pulling them apart. Did that mean that all Rivane boats were like this one, running on a fuel he couldn't see, singing songs beyond hearing?

"And every keeper is Bound," the captain muttered, so low that Wil wasn't sure she'd intended the words for him. And though she didn't speak it, an accompanying phrase formed in his mind.

Like every captain.

Or had he actually heard that? Had something whispered it in his ear or mind?

Wil lifted his eyes from the snarl of rope to where the green boat drifted ahead of them. Two cats sat on *Cloud Dancer's* bow. A third lay between them.

Three gray cats, all slightly different shades.

Was that all of them, or were there more?

Snatches of song from the green boat drifted back past them, and the cats' ears and noses twitched as if they heard or scented something interesting.

The captain grunted behind him, sounding pleased.

"What is it?" he asked.

"The sign on the right bank."

Wil's gaze shifted to the towpath. He couldn't see any obvious signposts. Unless…?

"The rocks?"

Two head-sized rocks lay on the far side of the towpath, marking a gap in the hedgerow that masked the field beyond. There was a blue symbol scrawled on one rock.

"Rivane marks for water," the captain said. "We need some. Fetch the pails."

The Tea Dream

Wil lay on the cot with the diary clutched to his chest. He'd had few opportunities to examine it in his weeks aboard *Cloud Dancer*, snatching a glimpse here and there when the captain left the boat. But he was never sure when she would return, and he knew he needed time to devote to examining the book's enigmatic pages. When he'd returned with yet another load of water earlier, he'd noticed how worn the captain looked—eyes shadowed, skin dry and gray. Even the orange in her hair had faded to a dull brass. Until that moment, he'd never considered her to be truly old.

An icy rain was falling, and she'd told him to empty the water into *Cloud Dancer's* tanks and check the mooring lines before turning in. By the time he'd entered the cabin, shivering and sniffling, she'd disappeared into her cabin, her exhaustion suggesting this was his chance to examine the diary. He'd still pulled blankets up around him and placed the lantern so he could dip the book into shadow if she emerged.

And then he had begun.

Page after page of drawings, snatches of poetry or songs in two, maybe three languages. Sketches of three curly-haired boys and a man who was a larger version of them. The father, perhaps? Did they look familiar? Scenes of canal life, of clouds and balloons drifting above landscapes. A third of the way through the book, a sketch sprawled across two pages. The subject was an old woman, older than the captain, with fathomless dark eyes and a cruel twist to her lips. While the other drawings were simple things, rendered quickly with a light, playful touch, the markings that made the old woman were dark, almost savage, ink bleeding on the page. The black eyes in the sketch held his, drew him down, and in, and…

In the dream, he was at the well again, pulling up the second pail in the fading afternoon. A leaf fell from a nearby tree into the pail. It was a dry thing, gray and brown, patchy from long exposure to wind and rain and snow, held together by the remnants of veins. Wil darted a hand into the water to fish it out, only to have it break apart, some pieces of the leaf drifting on the surface, others sinking. His fingers dove again, the water frigid on his skin.

Then a girl started sobbing.

From deep in the well.

Wil yanked the bucket up and set it beside the well, dipping his head deeper inside.

"Hello?" he called, the word echoing back to him.

Why had that been his initial impulse? Shouldn't he have been afraid?

The sobbing continued, but it was inside his head now, and fear was taking hold. Wil froze, his head still dipped into the well, muscles rigid.

There was never any girl, he told himself. You fetched the water and brought it back without incident this afternoon. This never happened. It's just in your head. A false memory. A trick your mind is playing on you.

He knew he was inside a dream now, that he had fallen asleep reading the diary of pictures and poetry. A desperate thought tugged at him, demanding attention. He needed to wake up lest the captain catch him with the book. Why? He'd found it. Wasn't he entitled to read it? As he thought this, he knew she would not want him reading it.

But why?

And then he was blinking, staring at black tea leaves sinking through amber liquid in a small porcelain cup. His fingers were not his own. They were a woman's fingers, but not delicate like his mother's. These were more like the captain's, nails trimmed short, decorated with callouses and small scars. Working fingers, not made to hold refined objects like this tea cup.

He looked up, and his heart went cold.

Cold within cold.

The woman whose body he was riding inside was terrified as well.

Of the old woman. The one from the diary sketch. She held something out to him.

To them.

A small packet.

"Blend it with his normal tea," the old woman croaked, eyes like a moonless night. "And he will sleep." Her chuckle was like gravel crunching underfoot. "Oh yes, he will sleep ever so deep. Then come to me with your sons, and I will spirit you away from him. He will never hit you or them again. You will be free."

Wil felt his fingers—the woman's fingers—clutching the packet, feeling the dry leaves inside and the hope they held. The old woman was lying about something. He knew that, and the woman he was inside of knew that. But to be away from her husband and his rages, the black mood that settled on him whenever he lost out on a job, or something went wrong with their boat, or one of their boys got in trouble, or he exchanged too many of their infrequent coins for a bottle.

"He will sleep," the old woman hissed, her chest rumbling with glee.

Wil sank into other dreams beyond remembering.

20

Almost As If She Were Sulking

The sky was leaden gray, and the wind seemed in a hurry to get from beneath it, rippling the water of the canal and blowing full in Wil's face as he stood beside the captain on *Cloud Dancer's* aft deck. She'd allowed him spells at the tiller today despite his oversleeping and almost missing out on helping her cast off this morning.

The cats had woken him, scratching at the door to be let out, and Wil had rolled from the cot and stumbled for the door, fumbling with the improvised string belt holding up his borrowed trousers. They were too large, but were better suited to life on a canal boat than anything in his suitcase. He'd pushed open the door and emerged into a sullen morning, only to find the captain awake and busy untying *Cloud Dancer* from her mooring. He'd rushed to help, apologizing and wondering why she hadn't woken him.

No explanation. No dressing down.

The opposite, in fact.

She'd offered him a chance at the tiller, sharp eyes watching his every move. He'd tried not to flinch when his grip shifted on the tiller, the boat's song changing pitch in response. To what end, Wil didn't know. One time, he'd attempted to reach for the gear throttle, but the captain had slapped his hand away with shocking speed. She hadn't even been looking at his hand. How had she sensed his intentions? Did the boat speak to her as it tried to speak to him through the song?

As he watched the banks drift by and thought of the throttle and the engine it controlled, Wil's eyes tracked along the towpath. Of course, everyone knew men or horses dragged canal boats of old. That's why the towpaths existed. But that was before coal powered boats, before the Rivane arrived. He twitched the tiller, easing the boat to the center of the canal. Beneath his feet, the engine throbbed. But no coal fired this engine. Why did no one question what was powering the Rivane boats?

Did anyone besides the Rivane care?

The gusting wind carried snatches of music to Wil's ears, music that wasn't coming from *Cloud Dancer*. Ahead, the green boat clung to the bank. The man with the white hair cradled an instrument on the aft deck, strumming and singing, shielded from the wind by the bulk of his boat.

"That's no Rivane song," he mused, and the captain grunted beside him.

"But the boat…?" Wil trailed off, unsure of what he was trying to ask.

"His wife was Rivane," the captain said.

Wil glanced at her, certain that there had been some emotion coloring the admission, but her face was a blank mask.

"Was?" Wil asked, uncertain how far to push her. They spent their days in silence unless she was instructing him about some function of the boat. Why was she so eager to share with him all the minute workings of *Cloud Dancer*?

"Died a dozen years back," she said.

"Long time to be alone," Wil said absently, wanting to take it back when the captain stiffened beside him.

They passed the green boat, an icy silence between them, cocooned by the white-haired man's strumming and low, wordless singing. When Wil twitched the tiller to move them further from the green boat, *Cloud Dancer* responded more sluggishly than she had at any point that morning, almost as if she were sulking.

21

The Cold Damp of a Colorless Market Town

For a market town, Linnister was surprisingly colorless—gray upon gray and shrouded in freezing mist. The few trees scattered amongst the buildings clawed at the sky with bare limbs. Somewhere beyond the buildings lay hills, presumably featuring something green or brown decorating their sides, but Wil saw them only as vague shadows fading in and out with the mist. He hitched the leather strap of the satchel further up his shoulders and made his way along Canal Street.

Every town they moored at had a Canal Street, the grubby, unloved step-sibling of the High Street packed with its inns and shops and cafes. Canal Street was always a practical place, providing provisions for the canal boats and shops to sell the goods those boats delivered. It formed a buffer between the Rivane and the monied classes, though the shopkeepers who manned that buffer sneered at the Rivane they had to do business with, ashamed by association. Not all, but most.

Wil pushed up the brim of the shapeless waterproof hat he'd scrounged from *Cloud Dancer's* closet of castoffs. The captain had been gone when he'd woken this morning, but she'd left a shopping list on the galley counter and a pile of coins. He'd done what he could to tidy the interior of the boat, gobbled down some tea and biscuits, and pushed out into the freezing mist, conscious of the small irony that this would have been the last week of winter break. In another world, a servant would have accompanied him on the short train journey to Isleywich to visit the booksellers and purchase supplies for the next term at Harlebone. Now he shivered in the cold damp of a colorless market town, hunting down boat supplies and lugging them home on his own.

Wil missed a step and stumbled at the thought. Was *Cloud Dancer* home for him now? Shaking off the strange thought, he shouldered his way into a shop marked with a coil of rope. Literacy was rare among the patrons of Canal Street. Wil tried not to feel the twinge of regret as he thought of what his literacy had bought him in his limited interactions with the Rivane of late. They would accept him in inns and at Gatherings despite his accent and coloring, valuing the fact that he could read and do figures for them, but as soon as they found out what boat he was from, a wall came down. They still treated him with politeness, but any warmth was gone.

Why? Was it something about the boat or the captain?

"What you want, river rat?" The shopkeeper squinted at Wil from his stool behind the counter and didn't look inclined to get up.

For a moment, Wil considered putting on the airs of his upbringing, donning his aristocratic armor to chastise the man for his rudeness.

But no. That wasn't him anymore.

"Mooring line. Two long coils."

The shopkeeper grunted and grudgingly pushed up from his stool to vanish into the storeroom behind him. Wil fished out the captain's list when he'd gone, sneaking a furtive glance at the paper before stuffing it back in his pocket. No sense in letting the shopkeeper know he could read. It'd be easier to catch the man trying to cheat him on the bill.

"A dozen pins too," he said as the shopkeeper emerged with the rope.

The man muttered something disparaging and vanished into the storeroom again.

Behind Wil, the bell on the door tinkled.

He didn't turn, but sensed the figure come up beside him and prayed that the presence was real.

"Is he in the back?" a familiar voice asked, and Wil's heart skipped a beat, crashing back hard against his ribs. He tilted his head away, hoping the boy beside him hadn't seen his face. Would the rags he was wearing be enough of a disguise? How could he get out of here without being recognized?

22

Four Months Ago in the Harlebone Library

The invader in Wil's hidden corner of the library was small and dark and sniffling quietly to himself, shoulders trembling behind the heavy tome that shielded his face. Wil had claimed this place on the second day of term, nearly three weeks ago now, and hadn't had to deal with a single intruder since. So who was this interloper?

Did it matter? He'd lost his haven. Time to retreat and find another. He took a step back, but the sickness that gripped him since he'd first stepped foot within the walls of Harlebone chose that moment to make him cough.

The tome dipped.

Eyes blinked, owlish behind the sturdy frames of unfashionable spectacles. Bits of black hair stuck out at improbable angles.

Scholarship boy. Must be with that hair and eyewear.

Wil's jaw clenched. He needed to go. Now.

His left foot took another step back, head already turning away when the boy let the book drop completely. Tears glistened on his bruised cheek. Blood welled from his cut lip.

Wil paused. For the briefest of moments, he'd thought the boy might be one of his ghosts, some specter of a Harlebone boy gone to an early and mysterious grave, his fate covered up by the masters and whatever group of aristocratic boys had tortured him into taking his own life, or worse, murdered him for sport or by accident.

"Stay," the boy whispered, his cut lip trembling.

Wil was powerless to resist, though he did not move closer.

At least the boy was real. Now that the initial shock of discovery was past, Wil vaguely remembered him from the dining hall, sitting alone, casting furtive glances at the boys gathered in laughing groups. Wil dined alone himself, but that was by choice. Whereas this boy…

"My name is Moske."

Strange name, stranger voice, hints of an accent that Wil could not place beyond a vague notion of the low counties in the Westlands.

"Wil," he said, not knowing why he replied. Every instinct told him to find some other corner of the library, to ignore the need in this boy's eyes. He twitched a glance down the aisle of bookshelves, aware that the other boys only tolerated his isolation because of his family. If they caught him fraternizing with a scholarship boy…

"This is your place," Moske said, setting the book down and pushing up from the chair. "I'll find another." He walked toward Wil, hunger in his eyes, his stance, his expression, all begging Wil to ask him to stop and stay.

Wil let him walk past, all quivering shoulders and hesitancy as their bodies brushed within centimeters of each other. It would be so easy to reach for the trembling shoulder, to offer to share this space of safety.

But easier to let him leave.

So he did.

Their paths would cross sometimes in the dining hall as the term progressed. Wil would wince at new bruises and the deepening hurt in Moske's eyes or the poorly repaired spectacles with one arm bent out of shape.

No words had passed between them since that day in the library.

23

All the Wrong Kinds of Attention

The shopkeeper emerged from the storeroom and quoted a price that was almost double what it should have been, but Wil was in no frame of mind to complain or bargain. He would reimburse the captain with the extra money in his suitcase. It wasn't like he'd paid for food or lodging.

Shielding his face from Moske, Wil moved to the counter, slapped down the coins, and shoveled the rope and mooring pins into the satchel without slipping it from his shoulder. He muttered his thanks in what he hoped was a passable Rivane accent, but the shopkeeper had already swept up his coins and moved on to Moske.

"What can I get you, sir?"

Sir? Wil almost allowed himself a smile. Moske was the same age as Wil, little more than a boy. But then, if Moske's people could afford the tutoring necessary to secure him a scholarship at Harlebone, they were likely among the wealthiest families in this town. Wil shook unkempt hair down to hide his features as he pushed past Moske, hunching in what he imagined was the subservient manner that Moske and the shopkeeper might expect of a lowly Rivane boy.

Almost safe.

Moske read items from a list, and Wil noticed how much more confident he was here in his own territory, among his own kind. It was an odd list. Ropes and sacks. Maybe his father was a merchant? Couldn't be too successful if he sent his son to haggle with shopkeepers rather than a servant.

Wil winced as he pulled the door open, the bell above thc door jangling.

That was when he made the mistake.

He turned to see if Moske had reacted to the noise and found the boy staring at him. Wil twisted back around and pushed through the door into the street. Not running. Running wouldn't be safe. A running Rivane boy with a full satchel would attract all the wrong kinds of attention.

But he needed to get away quickly.

Because Moske had seen his face.

Wil had seen the recognition blossom there, shifting Moske's features from frown to puzzlement to uncertainty to surprise. Wide eyes. A slight smile. Lips parting to…

To what?

To ask Wil why he was wearing Rivane rags, what he was doing in this provincial canal town in the remote Westlands?

Wil shrugged the satchel's strap further up his shoulder, head ducked forward, back hunched in expectation of Moske's shouts chasing him down Canal Street. But no shouts ever came, and Wil wasn't sure whether to be disappointed or relieved.

24

A Miasma of Animal
Sickness in the Air

Wil stepped across the gap from the Linnister mooring to *Cloud Dancer's* aft deck, shoulders tensing as always when the boat's song enveloped him. He glanced at the other Rivane boats moored nearby. Half a dozen, including the green boat belonging to the tall, white-haired musician, though no Rivane were visible. Small wonder, given the weather. Wil shook his head and descended the steps to the cabin doors.

They were unlocked, of course. Rivane did not lock their boats. Just another curious custom that Wil could not understand. He supposed the Rivane trusted each other to keep an eye out for intruders and outsiders when they moored together, but that didn't explain why they kept their doors unlocked when mooring alone in the countryside. He paused on the bottom step, eyes drifting to the hatch that concealed *Cloud Dancer's* engine. Was it his imagination, or was that where the song originated from? Could the strange presence he associated with the boat explain why Rivane security was lax? Did they trust their boats to mind themselves?

He shivered and twisted the handle, pushing into the cabin with the satchel already half off his shoulder when the smell inside the boat hit him. The shock made him stagger and caused him to draw a deep breath of fetid air before he could stop himself. There was a miasma of animal sickness in the air.

Could a cat have died?

Or maybe the captain?

Wil's heart lurched in his chest, pulse skittering and leaving him nauseated.

The captain's age was hanging heavier upon her with each passing day. What would he do if she was sick? Or worse, what if she was dead? Who could he go to for help? What responsibility did he have? He still had the money in the suitcase. He could just leave, walk away from *Cloud Dancer* and the canals.

Couldn't he?

The satchel slipped to the floor with a loud crash that set the small hairs on the back of Wil's neck on end. "Hello?" he called, taking one hesitant step into the cabin, followed by another. His fingers trailed along the galley counter, and he suppressed a shudder at the sense that it was warm to the touch, that the boat itself was a living thing. Could the boat have died rather than something inside of it? Was that the source of the smell? Was there a faint heartbeat radiating up through his fingertips?

Wil sniffed at the thick air again, wondering how much of the smell was real. Memories surfaced of Leeth, his eldest brother Hal's old wolfhound, dead these last three years. She'd been missing for two days when Wil stumbled into a broken old boathouse by the lake, hoping to find some place to be alone, away from his father's maniacal ranting, his mother's sobbing, Hal's poisonous glaring.

The air in the boathouse that day had possessed the same stench that now haunted *Cloud Dancer*. Animal sickness. Decay. The lurking specter of death.

Wil shook his head, trying to clear the ghosts of the past as he crept along the hall to the captain's chamber. His hand came up, knuckles ready to rap on the polished wood of the door. Instead, he reached for the handle and twisted, pushing the door open.

The portholes were covered, leaving the room submerged in gloom. The stench was even thicker here, but there was no sense of anything alive in the room.

Was the smell real?

Was she dead?

If so, would the blame fall on him? Would Moske see the constables dragging him away and enjoy a brief period of popularity at Harlebone as he related the tale of Wil's disgrace and arrest?

Wil crossed to the nearest porthole and removed the bung that blocked out the light. His neck resisted his instructions to turn, to see what was in the bed. Jaw clenched, he forced his entire torso around instead.

Empty.

The corners of the captain's bed were sharper than anything he'd seen at Harlebone, military in their precision. The rest of the room was neatly ordered. Papers stacked under a logbook on the small desk. Rolls of maps and charts in a barrel next to the desk.

Wil's legs grew watery, and he sank down on the bed, conscious that he was violating the captain's personal space, but unable to keep himself upright any longer. His fingers gripped the thick fabric of the folded quilt as something pressed down on him. Not one thing. Multiple presences. Phantoms. He could feel them moving through the space, brushing against him, their voices reaching his ears, but muffled so he couldn't make out the words. His wandering gaze fixed on something hanging from a hook in a shadowy corner of the room.

Goggles?

Flight goggles?

Ben had owned a pair of those, had been proud to show them off to Wil before...

Before bullets snatched his plane from the sky and scattered the machine across a foreign battlefield.

Along with Ben's broken body.

Why would a boat captain need pilot's goggles? And why was he so tired?

The air thickened, pushing Wil's cheek down against the quilt, leaving him staring at the planks on the wall, the blocked portholes. He blinked and struggled to open his eyes again. Something was sitting on his chest. A cat? But nothing had moved. Nothing was alive in here except him. The smell was oppressive.

The smell that might not be real.

Singing filled his ears and grabbed hold of his thoughts, dragging him down, down, down…

25

The Balloon Dream

The boat was *Cloud Dancer*, only it wasn't *Cloud Dancer*. Not yet.

Wil couldn't see the outside of the hull, but he knew it was deep crimson. Thoughts skittered, then aligned. He wasn't the one who knew the paint color, was he? It was her again. The one whose head he was a passenger in. The woman from his dreams.

Was he dreaming of her, or was she dreaming of him?

Strangely, the woman could hear the crimson boat singing, and Wil could hear it through her. That provided another clue for Wil. It wasn't *Cloud Dancer's* song she heard.

A pause.

Realization.

This woman could actually hear the boat's song. It wasn't just in Wil's head alone. Did she bear the same corruption of the mind that he did, or did all Rivane hear them?

Boat songs.

The woman blinked.

Wil blinked.

They stared at the sky together, arms aching from the washing they'd been slaving over for the past few hours. Her clothes. Her three boys' clothes. The witch's clothes.

How she hated the witch.

The old crone had lied to her. She'd given her husband the tea and waited for him to sleep, but then his face had turned white, then blue, then purple. He'd keeled over on the floor of their boat, not breathing.

It hadn't taken her long to decide what needed to be done. It wasn't as if she had any real options. She'd gathered her boys, shoved what they could carry into any bag she could find, and ran to the witch.

As the witch had known they would.

She'd been waiting, her mooring lines already cast off. A spider waiting patiently in her web.

Now she was a slave to the old woman, cleaning and cooking and running errands. Worse, she was certain that the old woman was teaching her boys to pickpocket at Gatherings.

Stealing from their own kind.

Shameful.

But what choice did they have? They were trapped. Who could she run to? No Rivane would help them—they were the witch's business. And the authorities of Saxe-Colraine? They would happily throw her in prison. Not for the murder of her husband but for the crime of being poor and Rivane and unable to support herself or her children.

Clouds scudded across the blue sky, and she envied them their freedom. Free to roam where they wanted, unconfined by canals and accidents of birth, by lack of money or better options, by this cold and gray country.

Something bright flashed behind a cloud, and she shaded her eyes, trying to make it out. Whatever it was moved with the wind. Wil knew, but he couldn't communicate with her. He was a mere passenger in her head, in a dream, in a memory.

The balloon emerged from behind the clouds, striped yellow and red, the basket dangling beneath canted at a severe angle as the wind's savage fingers clawed at it. The woman drew a sharp breath. Neither of them could see the person in the basket, but that didn't keep the woman from feeling envious of the flyer. Nor did it keep her envy from poisoning Wil's heart.

Freedom.

What she wouldn't give for it.

What he wouldn't give for it.

26

A Pale Face Painted with Moonlight

Wil came awake with a jolt that propelled his body off the bed, legs trembling like a newborn colt's. He scrambled for consciousness, the remains of the dream pulling apart like sodden paper. Silver moonlight came through the porthole, bathing the bed, winking off the goggles dangling beside it.

Goggles.

Balloon.

Clouds.

Wil shook his head as the dream released its hold on him, trying to remember what had woken him. Had it been the sudden crash or someone calling his name?

Crash?

Wil stumbled from the captain's cabin and past the washroom. The door to the deck was open, and a cat was mewling for his attention somewhere. Had it knocked something over? He reached the galley and looked down.

The captain sprawled on the floor, two cats nudging at her shoulders, a third staring up at Wil. For a long moment, he thought she was dead, and his mind raced along the probable future paths. Going for help and getting blamed for her death. Hal and his mother and the family lawyers descending. Or maybe vanishing into the night with his suitcase, finding a train station, and making his way at long last to the Smoke and Ben's grieving Callie. Or putting the captain on the bed and pushing the boat into the canal, letting *Cloud Dancer* take her body where it would.

The captain shuddered and drew breath, and Wil sank down beside her with relief. He rolled her over. Fever-bright eyes stared up at him from a pale face painted with moonlight.

"Bed," she hissed.

"I can run for a doctor. I have money."

Her head twitched, eyes picking out a bag on the floor nearby. "Already been. Powder in the bag. Mix with water. Bed first."

Wil nodded and lifted her, shocked both by how light she was and by his own strength. He'd never been much of an athlete, but life on the canal had piled ropey muscle on his thin frame. The cats twined through his legs as he carried her back to her cabin, depositing her on a quilt still wrinkled from where he'd inadvertently fallen asleep on it. Not that the captain would notice in her condition. Wil removed her boots and pulled the quilt over her, then darted back out to the galley to grab her bag and fill a mug with water, not caring if it was clean.

By the time he returned, the captain was breathing easier. Her eyes were open, glittering as they watched him approach. Wil knelt beside her and fished one of several small packets from the bag as she took the mug from him.

"Are you sick?" he asked, needing to say something, no matter how inane.

But the captain did not answer. She took a sip from the mug, then plucked the packet from his fingers, shaking its powdery contents into the water. Her gaze held him the entire time. She lifted the mug and drank more deeply, her throat working as it struggled to get the water and medicine down. Was it medicine? She hadn't said. His instinct was to reach for her, cradle her neck, encourage her to swallow, but he couldn't move.

She lowered the mug, and Wil grabbed it before the remains

spilled on the bed. "Tomorrow," the captain whispered. "If I'm not awake, cast off at first light."

"And then what?"

The captain's lips moved, shaping something that might have been, "She'll help you," though Wil couldn't be certain.

"Help with what?" Wil asked. "Who?"

But the captain's eyes fluttered closed, and her head sank back to the pillow beneath her.

"Who will help me?" Wil whispered to the sleeping captain.

27

Not Like Clearing the Weed Hatch

The next morning found Wil kneeling on the aft deck beside the hatch that concealed *Cloud Dancer's* engine. A cat crouched beside him, rubbing its head against Wil's thigh, and he scratched behind its ears in a way they all seemed to like.

"Right," he muttered. "You've waited long enough."

The captain had said to cast off at first light, but Wil had taken his time this morning, making unnecessary noise while getting dressed and putting the kettle on. Guilt gnawed at him. She'd been a wreck last night, and waking her up before she'd had a chance at a proper rest wouldn't help matters. But then, he'd never started *Cloud Dancer* on his own before. He'd watched her do it, true, but she'd never explained what she was doing and why. How did she think that prepared him to do it alone?

He could cast off the mooring lines and pilot the boat, but what about all that arcane muttering and hand gesturing he'd witnessed from Rivane lock keepers and the captain? How was he supposed to do that without instructions? That was akin to magic, wasn't it? Not like clearing the weed hatch or filling the water tanks.

So he'd banged his way about the galley while preparing his breakfast, making far too much noise while getting dressed and washing up. Then he'd stood for ages outside the captain's door, hoping she would wake and rescue him from his doubts.

"Do you know how to start it?" he asked the cat, glancing down into amber eyes.

The cat only yawned in response.

"Suppose not."

He drew a deep breath and reached for the hatch, scrunching up his face, waiting for the song drifting in the back of his mind to change from sleepy to alert and aggressive.

Maybe even angry.

But all he felt when his fingers brushed the metal catch was a slight piquing of interest, a muted eagerness on the boat's part.

"You want to go?" he whispered, and wondered why he did so. Was this why the Rivane were always whispering to their machines? Did something about the interaction prompt such intimacy? Wil frowned. "Talking to machines," he muttered. "Talking to cats."

The cat rolled onto its back and stretched.

"No offense, friend."

The catch popped with little effort, almost like it was waiting to be released, and Wil lifted the hatch. *Cloud Dancer's* song washed over him, pulling him forward, and he leaned over the engine, staring at an assemblage of gears and pipes and tubes that didn't resemble any machine he'd ever seen on a train or the farming equipment at his family's estates.

"And how would one start this mess?"

The cat rolled over and stood on its hind legs, putting both front paws on the open hatch and staring at the engine with him. It glanced up, expectant.

Wil shrugged. "How should I know? I was hoping it would be obvious. Figured it must be if she told me to start it. Maybe she forgot she didn't show me?"

The cat mewed and dropped down, slinking up the steps to the deck.

"Figure I'll be here a while, eh?"

Wil stared at the enigmatic engine, waiting for something to become obvious. There were glass gauges, metal pipes, black flexible tubes, but nothing that looked like a switch.

"Wouldn't be as simple as asking you to start, would it?"

He asked as a joke, but the boat responded, the engine throbbing to life. Black tubes twitched. Brass fittings vibrated. Wil looked at his left hand, the knuckles white where he gripped the hatch. He didn't realize he was holding his breath until he let it out in a long hiss.

"Right."

He dropped the hatch back into place above the engine and pushed upright, shading his eyes as he looked back east along the canal. Nothing coming. Time to cast off.

28

Blue Like the Sky

Cloud Dancer throbbed beneath Wil's feet and sang in his ears. His touch on the tiller was an afterthought, as if piloting the boat had less to do with steering than with whatever connection the song established between them.

The morning was fine, bright but chilly in the way late winter days sometimes were. Absent were the gray damp and biting winds he'd become used to. How many hours had they been cruising? It was hard to tell. Wil enjoyed losing himself in the journey. He watched the banks and occasional boat drift past, smiled at the birds swimming and diving, squinted at the beasts in the distant fields.

And the aeroplanes.

He shaded his eyes, daring to watch them again, to remember Ben's hands, long pointer and pinky extended on both, darting and diving around each other as he described flying with his squadron and the rush of wind in his hair and face, his stomach lurching as the wind bucked him, as the bottom dropped out when he put his machine into a dive.

"You've loved a pilot."

Wil jumped, teeth snapping together hard on his tongue. He

tasted salt before the inevitable spike of pain hit. Grimacing, he looked down.

The captain was in the doorway at the bottom of the footwell, staring up at him, a curious expression on her face lingering somewhere between sadness and amusement. She looked old and worn, skin papery and hair dull, but her blue eyes were sharp. Blue like the sky.

"I..." Wil trailed off, not knowing what to say, and the captain didn't seem eager to fill in the awkward silence that followed. Instead, she climbed the steps, legs trembling, hands darting constantly to provide support and stability.

"My brother," he managed at last when she reached him.

The captain grunted and squinted at the trio of flying machines darting around each other in swoops and spirals. Two yellow, one blue. "I remember the first balloons," she said, her voice faint. "I knew I needed to get in one, knew better than to ask Father."

Father.

Such a simple word, but the gravity she gave it was familiar to Wil. He knew the taste of the word and all that it entailed. The expectation. The guilt. Fear of failure. Disappointment. A sudden, stabbing sense of kinship set his eyes prickling with potential tears.

"It was months before he found out. Some peacock at the club, probably. I never learned who told him."

The goggles. Wil pressed his throbbing tongue against the back of his teeth. The goggles were the captain's. She'd flown balloons. But how long ago?

The captain clucked at him, and Wil started, saw that they were drifting close to the bank.

"Do you...?" He stepped aside, offering her the tiller. "Can you...?"

She frowned and took up her normal position, steering them back to the middle of the canal with a deft touch. Wil felt like an idiot and grasped for something to keep her talking.

"Is it similar?"

The frown didn't leave her face. Instead, it deepened. She shook her head.

"Two directions only. No up or down. No freedom."

"Freedom," Wil repeated softly. That was Ben's word, the one he'd used repeatedly. The freedom offered by the sky, or freedom from family chains? Wil closed his eyes and saw the scar that bisected Ben's left eyebrow, remembering his brother's face covered in blood after a childhood fall from a pear tree. He'd been ten or eleven years old and had climbed higher than Wil could ever imagine climbing before a branch cracked and gave way beneath him, sending him plummeting to the earth, laughing and screaming at the same time.

Ben could never get high enough or close enough to the sky.

Until he did.

Until that damned machine took him far higher than any pear tree ever could.

And came apart when the bullets chewed it up.

Sending Ben crashing down to the frozen earth.

Had he been laughing or screaming that day?

"Better get the waterproofs," the captain said.

Wil glanced up at the sky and frowned. No clouds. What was she talking about? Why did they need waterproofs?

Her eyes twitched toward him, her mouth quirking up at the corner. "Tunnel's coming."

29

The Shadows Were Waiting
for Him

A quarter mile ahead, the canal vanished into the side of a hill, swallowed by a circular stone mouth. Wil squeezed his eyes tight and swallowed the sticky lump lodged in his throat, trying not to think about the weight of earth and stone piled atop the tunnel.

A tunnel they were going through.

"Lanterns," the captain said, but Wil didn't move.

Couldn't move.

Her boot caught him on the shin, and Wil gasped, turning a furious gaze on the captain. She tilted her head toward the three lanterns sitting atop the cabin roof. "One at the bow and one at the midpoint. Light them. I'll take care of the third."

Wil bit the inside of his lip and nodded. He grabbed two lanterns and clambered to the side of the boat. She'd shown him how to work the lanterns earlier, and he'd hidden the fact that he'd already stumbled upon their working weeks ago.

Or was it a month ago? Maybe two? Or even longer?

He was losing track of time.

Making his careful way along the side of *Cloud Dancer's* hull, Wil tried not to rush. He wanted to get the lanterns lit and return to the stern before they penetrated the darkness looming ever closer. His hand brushed the hook at the boat's midpoint, and he toggled the first lantern alight, hanging it from the hook. Then he scrambled forward to the bow.

The shadows were waiting for him.

Whispering.

He reached the bow and lit the lantern, almost dropping it in his haste to hook it on its bracket. Then he spun and hurried back along the side of the boat, racing to reach the captain before they entered the tunnel.

Not fast enough.

The darkness swallowed them faster than the boat was moving.

The reason the captain had called for waterproofs became obvious as water dripped from the stone ceiling above. Wil gulped and glanced up as he reached the stern. Lantern light glistened on damp stone. A drop fell and splattered on his cheek, and Wil brushed it away with a shaking hand. He settled in beside the captain and forced his gaze forward.

The two lanterns seemed impossibly far away and surrounded by jagged jaws of shadow. The stone walls and ceiling pressed in around them.

"Did you see the signal flag?"

Wil started as the captain's voice bounced back off the stone, embracing them, overloud in the confines of the tunnel.

"What?"

"Before we entered," she said. "There was a green metal flag beside the entrance. It flips to red if another boat is already in the tunnel coming the opposite direction."

Wil nodded. It made sense. The tunnel was too narrow for two boats to pass.

"Are there runners?" he asked. It would be a miserable job to run back and forth across the hill to change the flags. Not to mention slow.

The captain chuckled, and he glanced at her.

"No," she said, but didn't elaborate.

Wil crossed his arms, pulling the waterproof tight around him. The woman was maddening. First, she sought to share her knowledge by telling him about the flags, but then she closed down when he pushed for more.

Shadows crawled along the wet stone, and Wil's teeth ground together. The whispers were growing louder. He allowed himself a moment to close his eyes, mouthing a prayer to a deity he had no faith in.

Cloud Dancer responded, her song swelling in his head to drown out the whispers. Wil's eyes snapped open. Had the boat heard his thoughts? How much longer would the darkness last?

"Quarter of the way through," the captain said.

Could she hear his thoughts as well?

Wil gripped the rail that enclosed the stern deck, hand clenched so tight it hurt. He couldn't shake the feeling they were descending into the depths of the earth. Logic told him the canal had to remain level to keep the water from flooding out, but logic didn't hold sway here. Not beneath tons of rock and dirt, surrounded by darkness and the endless drip, drip, drip.

Who turned the flags?

More Rivane magic?

Where was the sky?

"Halfway," the captain muttered.

A spot of light appeared beyond the bow lantern, and Wil twisted to look behind them, spotting another point of light in the darkness.

His jaw ached with tension, and the pulsing behind his eye was making the lid twitch and his eye sting. He faced forward again and willed the spot of light that was the tunnel exit to grow, for the sky to come embrace him.

30

Her Eyes Were Bright and Still

Wil clambered along *Cloud Dancer's* hull and snatched up the coiled bow line, stretching the kinks from his back. He'd spent the duration of their trip through the tunnel hunched over and had to force himself upright at the end. So much mud and rock held back by so little stone. All of it ready to collapse and bury the canal, bury them.

Wil shivered and prepared to jump, eying the muddy bank, hoping the captain could bring the boat in close enough that he didn't risk an ignominious splash back into the cold water of the canal. It had been weeks since he'd last fallen in, and he didn't look forward to repeating the experience.

He glanced back at the captain. She'd been steadily declining since their exit from the tunnel, as if she'd been holding things together until they could navigate that nightmare passage. Her eyes were bright and still while the rest of her grew dull and quavery. She huddled beneath her battered hat and overcoat, still wrapped in the waterproof she'd worn in the tunnel despite the day turning pleasant.

After exiting the tunnel, they'd navigated a single lock with little help from the lock keeper. The keeper had been a woman this time, muttering to herself and ignoring Wil's half-hearted attempts at conversation. She'd been crying when they exited the lock, but the captain had offered no explanation, and Wil hadn't pressed the issue. They'd passed through a town shortly after, and the captain had been eager to dock, but the moorings were all taken. It wasn't a large town, and Wil wasn't certain what her business would be there, but she'd been insistent they find the next available mooring.

So here they were, about a half-mile past the town. He hoped she wasn't stubborn enough to insist on walking back to the town tonight. She needed her rest, and only half an hour of daylight remained.

Cloud Dancer bumped against the bank, jolting Wil from his reverie. He gripped the rope tight and made the short jump from bow to bank, boots sinking a few inches into the soft turf. For a moment, he swung his arms, scrambling for balance, getting his center of gravity shifted up the bank rather than back over the canal. He slogged through mud to the mooring post and tied the rope fast, then jogged toward the stern, where the captain stood waiting with the stern line.

Wil frowned. If he could have done it all himself, he would have. She should be abed. But he didn't have the experience or the knowledge to handle the boat by himself. Not yet.

He wondered at that thought.

Not yet? How long did he plan to stay on the canals?

The coiled line came arcing toward him and Wil snatched it out of the air, dragging *Cloud Dancer's* stern to the bank. Three gray shapes flashed off the boat and across the towpath, vanishing into the hedge.

"Good hunting, lads," he muttered as he tied off the stern line.

By the time he'd finished, the captain was already on the bank. Wil frowned at the plank she'd laid from stern to shore. She rarely used it unless the bank was especially muddy, and the area where the stern butted against the shore was dry compared to where he'd had to jump.

How much pain must she be in to require it?

"Should be back before nightfall," she muttered, every word an effort.

Wil opened his mouth to protest, then caught the glint in one blue eye peering from beneath the broad brim of her hat. He closed his mouth and nodded instead.

"Help Denny get moored," she said. "Then get some dinner on. He might join us."

"Who's Denny?"

The captain tilted her head back in the direction they'd come from, and Wil's eyes followed. The green boat that had sometimes been their companion on the canal was barely visible in the distance. He hadn't seen it for days.

How had she known it was there?

"Sure thing," he replied, but she had already turned away from him, shrugging a satchel up on one hunched shoulder and setting off along the towpath. Wil watched her for a long moment, tempted to rush after her and tell her to wait for morning, to insist on him running whatever errand seemed so urgent. But then he thought of that blue eye and held his tongue.

His eyes moved back to the green boat.

How much, he wondered, did Denny know about the captain?

31

Denny

Wil watched the green boat approach, noting the rhythmic catch in the soft chug of its engine, so different from *Cloud Dancer's* steady rumble. Each Rivane boat had a distinct voice, almost as if no two engines were the same. And beyond the noise of the engine…

A song. So faint that Wil wondered if he was imagining it.

Did Denny's boat have a song like *Cloud Dancer's*? Did all Rivane boats have songs?

Wil wasn't about to ask. He knew that not everybody could hear them, otherwise it would be general knowledge that Rivane boats sang. But he'd heard no such rumor. Was it all in his head? Like the voices and the visions? The dreams?

What if no one else could hear them?

Wil shivered as the two boats' songs brushed against each other, marking each other's presence, almost like pedestrians nodding as they passed in the street. He pushed back the limp hair falling across his eyes—when had it gotten so long?—and focused on the man piloting the boat.

Denny was long and lean, his white ponytail twitching over his shoulder as he glanced back along the canal. One hand floated near the tiller, but Wil wasn't sure Denny was touching it. He frowned at the song Denny was singing, trying to reconcile it with the boat's song. They didn't seem to have any harmony or melody in common, and yet they blended together somehow.

Did that mean Denny could hear his boat's song as well, or was Wil's mind just fabricating the boat's song and matching it to Denny's? The man's eyes drifted across Wil, and he lifted one hand to wave. Denny wore Rivane garb, but he looked about as Rivane as the captain. Too tall and too pale, with an aristocrat's hawkish features. If it weren't for his dress and hair, he'd have fitted into any dinner party Wil's parents might have hosted.

Back when they hosted dinner parties.

Before his father's fits became too intense and too frequent to hide.

Wil waved back and pointed to the mooring post beside him. Denny nodded and released the tiller, scrambling along the side of his boat with practiced ease to retrieve the bow line, singing all the while. Wil's gaze moved back and forth between Denny and the tiller, eyes narrowing as he noted the tiller was steady, almost like an invisible hand held it.

A coil of rope hissed through the air, demanding Wil's attention. His hand darted out to catch it, breaking the spell of the dueling songs. Dragging the line, Wil pulled the bow of the green boat to the edge of the canal, then wound the rope fast around the mooring post. Straightening, he turned to walk back and help with the stern line, but froze instead.

Denny stood at the edge of the stern deck with one line coiled around his shoulder and another already tossed to the bank. His hands weren't on the tiller, but the boat was angling itself toward the shore. Wil watched, mouth hanging open, as the boat steered itself against the bank. Denny leapt to shore and tossed a line in Wil's direction before tying off at the stern himself. Wil shook off his surprise and retrieved the line, tied it off. He looked up as Denny approached.

"Thanks for the help," the man said. Smooth, educated tones. Maybe Harlebone, maybe Ettings. The most exclusive schools imprinted themselves on the speech patterns of their pupils, marking them for recognition by others of their kind.

"Didn't seem like you needed it," Wil said, glancing back at the boat, still trying to work out how it had steered itself. He'd sometimes felt as if *Cloud Dancer* was making minor corrections herself while he was piloting her, but that had to be his imagination or some breeze or shift in the water from pounds being filled or drained at a lock.

Right?

"Name's Denny."

Wil took the offered hand. "Wil." No need for the heavy last name. Denny hadn't bothered with one. Doubtless, he bore a similar burden to Wil.

Denny glanced at *Cloud Dancer*. "You've been with Val for what, six weeks? Maybe two months?"

Val? Was that the captain's name? How was he only learning it now?

Wait.

Two months? Was break over already? When would his family send someone to drag him back to Harlebone?

Wil coughed and scratched at his neck. "She went to town," he said, not knowing what else to say. "Said she would return by nightfall. I'm on dinner duty tonight. Will you join us?"

Denny nodded and grinned. "Harlebone?"

"Excuse me?"

Denny hooked a thumb at his chest. "I was a Naveriche boy."

Naveriche was on the south coast. Not quite in the same league as Harlebone or Ettings, but close.

"From your little speech there, I pegged you as a Harlebone, Cashtongray, or Ettings boy. Since we're riding this stretch of canal, I figured Harlebone was most likely."

Wil nodded. "I'm not going back."

Denny shrugged. "Your life, Wil. Got to get the old girl bedded down now, but I'll join you around nightfall. Have a couple of bottles gathering dust that I think Val will appreciate more than me."

He gave a half-wave and turned away. Wil watched him jump back aboard the green boat, then looked down as something bumped his ankle. A cat stared up at him.

"What do you want? Bad luck hunting?"

The cat seemed to shrug, then moved off along the towpath toward *Cloud Dancer*. Wil followed, glancing back at the green boat to see Denny crouched over his engine hatch, singing softly into it.

And the boat sang back.

Heat flooded Wil's cheeks. This was too intimate. He shouldn't be watching, shouldn't be listening…

Wil tripped over something. He staggered and caught himself, glaring at the cat that had twined through his legs.

"You trying to kill me?" he hissed.

But the cat just stared at him. Behind it were its two brothers.

All staring at him.

"What do you want?" he asked, the flesh prickling along his forearms. It was almost like they wanted to tell him something.

But cats didn't talk.

Did they?

32

The Crash Dream

Black-winged birds with the faces of Harlebone masters pursued Wil through a forest of brick and ivy. Their raw croaking grated at his ears. Their talons and beaks lacerated his flesh. He was running, staggering, stumbling…

Falling…

A scream enveloped him. His scream?

A smell devoured the scream.

An overpowering stench of rotting vegetation.

Its jaws closed around him, shook him, dragged him into another dream…

Where he pulled arms plastered with slime from a weed hatch and gagged. He leaned over the canal, his stomach heaving.

He paused.

She paused.

Wil's reflection in the water was that of a Rivane woman, small and dark with eyes like embers. Wil fought the urge to duck from her sight, knowing this was a memory. There was no possibility of her seeing him behind her eyes.

Or could she?

The woman looked up at a sudden burst of excited shouting to see her three sons crashing through the hedge that bordered the towpath. Little criminals. No doubt they'd been raiding the neighboring fields. She had little control over them now—they were the witch's creatures through and through. Liars and thieves, though they still bore her a strange loyalty she did not understand.

"Mother," shouted Umal, the eldest. "Come see. A balloon in the field."

"Balloon?"

"It crashed. Dragged for a full two hundred yards if it were an inch." That was from Tiray, the youngest.

"Is this a joke?" She directed the question to Duzet, the middle child and the one least likely to lie to her. Or hide a lie from her.

He nodded, eyes bright, forehead shiny with sweat, little black ringlets of hair plastered to his cheeks, reminding her uncomfortably of his father.

Hands raised, the three boys beckoned to her.

"Come," Umal insisted.

She straightened, kicking the hatch closed as she grabbed a rag and wiped the slime from her arms. The witch would wake soon, no doubt in a cross mood. If she couldn't place the blame on the boys' shouting, she'd find some other fault to pick at. But maybe she could be appeased with something scavenged or stolen from the crashed balloon.

A sharp sigh. An agile leap across the gap to the bank.

"Come on then," she said to her boys.

They dragged her through the hedge and into the field beyond, nudging, pushing, and pulling. Ahead of them, ragged fabric twitched and snapped in the same wind that yanked at her hair. How hadn't she noticed a balloon going down? Her head had been buried in the hatch, but still…

No time for that now. She was running, leaving the boys and their shorter legs behind, drawn to the balloon. She'd only seen them as objects in the distant sky and never imagined being this close to one. What would the pilot be like? Likely young, pale, and handsome. Some terrible aristocrat. But what if he was hurt? Her bare feet flashed through scythed grass stalks, and she darted past hay bales stacked like pale fortresses lined up to repel invaders.

Invaders like her.

The rippling, striped fabric of the balloon tried to smother her as she ducked through it, tendrils of cloth curling round her arms and legs. "Get off," she muttered, then almost laughed as she realized she was talking to fabric. Behind her, the boys shouted with glee as they piled into the billowing mass.

Her eyes narrowed, darting to find the source of the moan that brushed her ears above the snap and rustle of fabric. She shifted her steps toward the sound, fighting through rippling walls of color to find the pilot sprawled beside the basket, head turned away from her and covered by a leather cap. Spots of red and brown stained the pale fabric beneath his torn jacket. Her roving eyes reached the pilot's legs, and she gasped.

One leg was bent at an unnatural angle below the knee, a dark patch of blood spreading through the soft brown trouser leg.

"Saints above and below," she murmured, sketching a Rivane ward of protection.

Was she too late?

She ducked down and tugged at the pilot's shoulder, turning him over.

Soft, pale features. A Saxer aristocrat, as she'd suspected. Delicate nose framed by a spattering of unexpected freckles. The lack of a beard didn't surprise her, but she had expected at least a mustache. Most Saxer men wore them.

The pilot's gloved hand pushed up the goggles to reveal cornflower blue eyes. Orange hair, bound in a thick braid, slipped from beneath the leather cap.

Braid?

The lack of facial hair and delicate features made sense now. The pilot was a woman.

"Think my leg's going to be out of commission for a while," she said through a grimace. She squinted up at Wil, at the woman Wil shared a body with.

Her narrowed eyes widened.
They were so blue.
And so very, very beautiful.
Like the open promise of the sky.

33

His Befuddled Mind Painted Blue

Wil woke to a darkness that his befuddled mind painted blue. Blue like the eyes of the balloon pilot in his dream. He swallowed. That had been the captain, only younger. The goggles in her cabin made sense now.

If the dreams were real.

Wil's left eye twitched and stung. It felt like some foreign mass had lodged there. He touched fingers to his burning temples, massaging them gently. What had Denny called the captain? Val? What traditional Saxer name would that be short for? Valouria? Valentia? What family could she claim?

And who was the woman whose eyes he had seen the captain through, whose memories he had been dreaming the past few weeks? Or was it months now? The woman was Rivane, that much was certain. And she'd fallen for the captain when she'd first looked in her eyes. Wil wasn't just seeing through the Rivane woman's eyes. He was part of her. Thinking her thoughts. Feeling her emotions. Living her memories. He'd felt her cheeks flush and her chest burn hot, her legs go watery and soft.

A scratching sound dragged him from his contemplation of the dream, and it took him a moment to remember where he was.

The cot.

On a Rivane canal boat.

The scratching came from the door to the aft deck. A cat, wanting to be let out. Is that what had woken him?

"Be there in a moment," he muttered, unfurling from the cot, stretching aching limbs and back and making his way in near darkness through the galley. Faint light crept through the drawn curtains on the galley window, providing just enough to see by, though Wil had much of the small boat mapped in his head now and could probably navigate it blindfolded.

He was reaching for the door handle when a voice froze him where he stood. Someone was talking, just on the other side of the door. Wil knelt, one hand brushing the door handle, the other questing for the cat he could hear purring in the darkness below him. A cold nose bumped his palm, and Wil traced back along the cat's skull, found the spot behind its ears they all seemed to relish. The purring intensified, but Wil wasn't paying the cat any heed. He pressed his ear to the door.

The captain was speaking. It sounded like she was arguing with somebody. But who? Denny? Maybe somebody from the town she'd been to visit today? Wil caught snatches of words and heard his own name. He sensed the shift in the captain's voice from conciliatory to cold to pleading. And all the while, the song he associated with the boat seemed to alter in response, accelerating when the captain's voice took on a harder edge, slowing and becoming more melodic as she soothed.

Wil held his breath. Were they communing? The captain and the boat?

He jerked upright, hand wrenching back from the handle as if it had burned him, ashamed of eavesdropping on such intimacy. He'd heard the raw emotion in the captain's voice. The sorrow.

And the longing.

The hatch closed with a clang, and Wil spun, flying back to his cot, hip jarring against the galley counter, though he strangled the curse that threatened to leap past his lips. He dove for the cot and pulled the quilt around his shoulders just as the door creaked open.

"I heard you," the captain said softly, and Wil's stomach went knotted and cold. He kept his eyes closed, and it took him one panicked moment to realize that her words were not meant for him.

The cat.

She was talking to the cat.

She must have heard it scratching at the door.

Leather creaked, and the captain bit back a groan. Had she bent down to pet the cat? The door closed with a click, and she shuffled through the galley. Wil forced himself not to scrunch his eyes further shut.

She paused over him, and Wil pictured the woman in the crashed balloon, sprawled out of the basket, blood darkening the fabric of her trousers. How long ago had that been? What had happened to the woman whose dreams he shared, who had fallen for the captain at first blush?

But even as the question formed, he knew the answer, certainty solidifying as the captain's boots retreated to her room.

His dreams were not his own. He shared them with a presence he felt every day, whose song embraced him every waking hour and every sleeping one too. The one the captain communed with and consoled and argued with. The one whose journal he'd been reading in fits and snatches.

She was *Cloud Dancer*.

34

A Sense of Wrongness Hung
Heavy in the Air

Wil did not remember falling asleep. It seemed like he'd lain awake for hours after his midnight eavesdropping on the captain's communion with the boat, his thoughts tumbling over each other. He was aware of a change in the tone of *Cloud Dancer's* song, something he couldn't quite place, but that made him uneasy. And now, come morning, the quilt had twisted around his limbs, loath to release him. Was it an extension of *Cloud Dancer's* will, keeping him imprisoned?

His eyes tracked around the cabin. Gray light crept past the curtains, promising a drab day ahead. Rain pattered on the roof. Probably snowing up north.

Where he should be.

Or was he supposed to be back at Harlebone? Was break over? Time wasn't something he'd been keeping track of—days bled into each other on the canals. Were his classmates back at school? Did anybody miss him?

Wil struggled to free himself from the twisted quilt and slid his legs over the side of the cot, though he did not stand. Something was off. A sense of wrongness hung heavy in the air, leaving him light-headed and dizzy.

He braced and pushed to his feet, struggling to catch himself as his balance deserted him. Breath hissed through his teeth. One foot was numb, pins and needles stabbing through the sole. The timbre of the boat's song changed, almost as if it was expecting him to fall and eager to see it happen.

"No," he grunted, surprised by his own anger.

Twitching the gathered quilt around his shoulders, he staggered to the galley. He didn't look at the narrow passageway that led to the captain's chambers. He didn't need to. Somehow, he knew she was in there, still sleeping. He paused at the galley counter, blinking away the disturbing certainty he felt.

"Tea," he muttered, then looked at the door as a cat scratched at it.

From the outside this time.

The numbness had retreated from Wil's foot, so he took a few ginger steps to the door and pulled it open a crack. Three gray shapes slithered through the gap.

"All together then, boys?"

They belonged to the boat, belonged on it. They were as much a part of it as the captain.

So what did that make him? Intruder or guest?

Thoughts of tea forgotten, he pushed the door open and climbed into a morning trapped somewhere between spitting rain and heavy mist. The neighboring mooring was empty. Denny must have pulled up stakes already. Wil frowned as images pushed into his head of the green boat drifting past in the gray dawn. The base of his skull throbbed, every pulse hammering the back of his head. A familiar feeling he'd suffered for years.

And not a welcome one.

"Tea," he muttered again, and turned back to the steps.

He stopped, frozen, one foot hanging over the first step, and stared at the engine hatch, remembering last night. The captain communing with the boat, with the Rivane woman he was dreaming of. He'd heard her say his name. Why?

Wil's fingers inched out to brush the metal hatch, tips tingling with the contact. Images of blue eyes behind goggles, balloons drifting unfettered, dirty boys pelting along the towpath, an ancient crone with beetle-black eyes, a man with curly hair and an angry glint in his eye.

A lump formed in Wil's throat, threatening to choke him. He lifted his hand from the hatch and pressed it to the throbbing base of his skull, willing the images away. The throbbing intensified, keeping time with his pulse, each beat slamming against his skull from the inside. He squeezed his eyes shut, swaying where he crouched, feeling the steps shifting beneath him, darkness reaching, clawing, grasping...

35

The Curse Dream

Pain in his head.

In his limbs.

His chest.

Everything hurt. But this wasn't Wil's pain. At least he didn't think it was. There was a gauzy distancing, a veil between him and the agony that tore through the woman. He was in her head again, in her body, suffering her pain at a slight remove.

Bearing witness to her memories.

Months had passed since the balloon crash. While she'd never forgotten the pilot with the blue eyes and the orange braid, she'd been careful to keep her thoughts shielded from the witch, to never think about her when the witch was around. She wasn't sure if the crone could read her mind, but she wasn't taking any chances. The memory was too precious. As was what that memory represented, what the woman with the blue eyes represented.

Freedom.

And then, a fortnight ago, a bicycle had come hurtling down the towpath at reckless speed. She'd glanced up from her washing, lancing the rider with a withering glare. It was doubtless some local youth, probably inebriated, uncaring for the safety of others who needed the path. She'd returned her eyes to the washing, only to whip her head back up when she processed the orange braid trailing out from beneath the rider's cap.

Fortunately, the witch had taken the boys to the market to dip their fingers into local pockets, leaving her alone for a few hours.

Leaving the two of them alone.

The woman with the braid was named Valorine—Val for short—and she offered a balloon ride as thanks for coming to her aid after the crash. It had taken this long for her broken leg to heal, but she'd tracked down the boat of her would-be rescuer while she was recovering.

Now here she was.

It was terrible.

And perfect.

Perfectly heartbreaking.

She tried to make Val understand why she couldn't leave the boat, why the witch could never find out about this visit. But then Val kissed her, and everything made sense.

Nothing made sense.

For two weeks, they managed clandestine meetings and stolen kisses behind the hedgerow.

Then the witch and the boys discovered them. They burst into the boat and found her and Val in an embrace.

The witch saw.

The boys saw.

She didn't know which was worse.

Val strode between them, shielding her from the crone, demanding her release from servitude, threatening legal action, solicitors, police, all the forces of law that an aristocrat could bring to bear. But the crone ignored Val. Her finger extended, and Wil felt her black eyes stabbing into the woman whose body he rode within.

"Ungrateful wretch," the crone snarled. "I saved you."

In exchange for life as a slave. That's what she should have replied, what Wil was trying to should through her. But her thoughts were impossible to reel in. Her mind raced, blood roaring in her ears. Without being conscious of doing so, the little knife she wore at her belt slipped into her hand, hidden behind her back.

The witch came forward, and Val stepped across her path. The balloon pilot was taller by far. And strong. She raised an arm to hold the old woman back, but the crone stared into her eyes and whispered a word of malevolence that twisted in the air like a snake before lashing out. Val dropped to the floor, screaming. The witch stood over her, a mingled look of victory and pleasure twisting her leathery visage. Her black eyes lifted.

The knife flashed forward.

She hadn't thought about it. Wil didn't understand what was happening until the blade was already burrowing through layers of fabric, seeking ancient flesh, seeking blood.

And flesh it found.

Blood it released.

The witch's blood was dark. It spurted and bubbled, black and polluted. The witch grabbed hold of the wrist that held the knife and dragged herself forward, whispering the words of a curse that sealed all of their fates.

Shaping words.

Killing words.

Binding words.

36

A Chill Gripped His
Rebellious Stomach

The first thing Wil felt was icy water on his fingertips. Then came the cold damp soaking his chest, legs, and arms. Sunlight bathed the left side of his face, painting his closed eyelid red-orange. He groaned and forced his eyes open, the lids parting with a sickening tearing sensation as the morning crust gave way.

The canal stretched out before him, empty save for a quartet of ducks in the distance. Frost rimed the grass crawling down the banks. His eyes tracked along his arm to where his fingers trailed in the water. Patches of ice floated on the surface nearby. Liquid everywhere. In the canal, the frost.

And then he remembered the dream and liquid of another sort.

The feel of the blade sliding through withered flesh and warm blood pumping over his hand. *Her* hand. The woman in the dream. She'd killed the crone. Or had that been him? Was he capable of murder?

Wil gagged and curled up on himself as his stomach heaved, pain lancing through his gut as the muscles worked with no effect. He had nothing to throw up but the stringy bile he spat in the frozen grass, stomach still performing its futile clenching.

The boat.

He shivered and rolled over. There she was. *Cloud Dancer.* A chill gripped his rebellious stomach. Was he relieved the boat had not left him, or was he dreading stepping aboard again?

He knew why the boat sang now, knew why she responded to the captain like she did.

The boat was cursed, a woman's soul bound to her engine.

Wil pulled his knees to his chest and gripped them tight, the chill in his gut spreading through his body, setting him quivering. Was that the Rivane secret? Locks and boats. Machines inhabited and powered by imprisoned souls. The sadness and distress Wil had witnessed amongst the Rivane made sudden sense. From the tears in Old Garfo's eyes to the intimacy of Denny's songs and the captain's melancholy, there was a logic to it all now.

A cat watched him from the stern of *Cloud Dancer.*

One of the three.

Also bound to the boat.

Cursed like their mother.

Wil closed his eyes and pressed his forehead to his knees. What had he gotten himself into?

He might have stayed like that for hours but for the sound coming up the towpath. A steady squeak, squeak, squeak of metal in need of oil. He turned his head, ear resting on his knee, and watched the bicycle and the man pedaling it. The man did not look like he belonged on the bicycle. Too well dressed, for one thing. Though the suit wasn't what an aristocrat or wealthy merchant might wear, the fabric had quality, and it fit well enough to suggest a decent tailor. The bowler hat and elaborate mustache didn't belong on a bicycle either. As the bicyclist came closer, Wil could see that he wasn't comfortable on the machine. He was sweating and so focused on maintaining his balance that he didn't even register Wil sitting on the bank.

Still, his eyes drifted up occasionally, and Wil saw his quick nod of satisfaction when he marked the boat.

He'd been looking for *Cloud Dancer.*

Was the captain still aboard?

Was it any of Wil's business?

The bicyclist rolled past, still unaware of Wil's presence at the edge of the canal. He pulled to a stop beside *Cloud Dancer's* mooring and leaned the bicycle against the post.

Wil drew a shuddering breath and stood.

37

Polidet Craine, Solicitor

The bicyclist removed his hat and applied a handkerchief to his sweaty brow. Dab. Dab. A conspicuous pause as he marked movement at the corner of his vision. Turning, he placed the hat back on his head and stared at Wil.

Waiting for him to approach?

Wil shoved his hands in the pockets of his too-large trousers and shuffled along the towpath, eyes darting from man to boat to the green verge that bordered the path, aware all the time of the man's eyes on him. What would he see? A ragged boy, tall for a Rivane. Hair the right shade but not curly. Skin too pale beneath the dirt. The mismatched clothes and unkempt hair might negate any suspicion he was anything other than one of the canal folk. And this man? What would he be? Not gentry. Not a merchant either. Most merchants substituted garishness for class, and this man's dress was more subdued than that. More likely a bookkeeper or something similar. Wil had encountered many of the sort in service to his family and recognized the man's professional air.

"I say, young man."

Wil glanced up. He hadn't realized how close he'd gotten to the bicyclist, though he should have. *Cloud Dancer's* song was stronger now. Was that how he had ended up along the canal this morning? Had the song driven him from the boat?

Wil stopped, slouching to further disguise his height, and stared.

A small frown creased the man's lips. Had he been expecting a more deferential greeting?

"This boat." An unnecessary tip of the bowler toward the only boat in sight. "It is called…" a slight hesitation, "*Cloud Dancer?*"

Wil nodded. The fewer words he spoke, the better chance he could disguise his accent and hide the fact he wasn't Rivane. Would this man even notice? Had Wil's dirtiness and clothes already defined him in the man's mind?

The man's gloved fingers twitched up to a fold in his coat. They paused.

"Is this your boat?"

Wil shook his head. True, he was a passenger and sort of crew on *Cloud Dancer*, but he would never claim that the boat belonged to him.

"You know the captain?"

Wil nodded.

"Is she aboard?"

Wil shrugged. An honest response. He suspected she was, but it wasn't a lie to say he wasn't sure. Maybe it was time to risk a few words? Trying to keep any aristocratic coloring from his speech, he adopted a rough whisper that he hoped sounded poor and foreign. "We don't lock up. Go in and see."

He said it knowing that a man like this wouldn't do so, that the very prospect would horrify him, that he probably double bolted his own doors and always experienced a moment's panic whenever he returned home, wondering if someone had broken in and violated the sanctity of his domain. It gratified Wil to see him shudder.

"No." The man looked from Wil to the boat and back again. "No, I think not." His eyes tracked up and down Wil's dirty frame. The gloved hand vanished inside the coat. "Can you deliver a message?"

Wil nodded again, not trusting his ability to hide his accent.

The man pulled a sealed letter from his coat. Wil's eyes glided over the seal. Fancy. Aristocratic. What connections did the captain have? Was this a hint of her old life? The man held out the letter, pinched between two gloved fingers, and Wil took it from him. Another dip into a pocket, and two coins followed the letter.

"Have you seen a boy on this boat?"

Wil froze.

"Maybe a few years younger than you?"

Thank heaven for the disguising power of dirt and ill-fitting clothes.

Wil let out his breath in a low hiss, hoping the man hadn't noticed his sudden stiffness. But the man had turned to regard the boat, his posture radiating disapproval. Wil twisted the letter in his hand, not daring to look down at it. If this man caught him reading, he might suspect...

"Well?"

The man was looking at him again, expectant.

"No," Wil grunted. He, personally, had never seen a boy on this boat, much less one a few years younger than him. Unless you were counting dreams, and that wasn't what this man was asking, was it?

"See that the boy gets the letter, will you? I'll expect him in town, today or tomorrow."

Wil must have given some response because the man sniffed and turned to retrieve his bicycle. Not that Wil remembered making any reply. Nor could he remember his last breath. He held it until the man mounted his machine and turned it around, setting off back down the towpath amidst a chorus of squeaks.

Not the captain.

The letter was for him.

When the sound of the bicycle faded, Wil let his breath out slowly. His eyes dropped to the envelope.

Master Wilstaire Cathermay-Gravence.

Care of Polidet Craine, Solicitor, Upper Misling Town.

The seal was his father's.

Wil broke it, angry but dreading what he would find inside.

38

In Every Awkward Ink Blot

Wil didn't know how long he stood frozen on the towpath. He clutched the letter in nerveless fingers, thoughts racing along potential timelines. Breaking the seal had been like an admission that he was just playing pretend here on the canals, that his real life lay behind that seal, within the walls of his family's estates. He'd only needed to read the first few words of the letter before his vision had gone hazy, the rest of the message rendered meaningless.

"Hal has had an accident. You must return."

His mother prided herself on her penmanship, and it was obviously her hand that had written the words. But in every misplaced swoop, in every awkward ink blot, Wil had read the message the Slirentha Billingray Cathermay-Gravence had not intended to send. She was frayed and desperate. If she was writing to Wil, that meant his eldest brother Hal was dead or on the brink of death. What sort of accident?

The derailed train of Wil's thoughts went even further down the bank, smashing through little hillocks of hope and plans for the future. He saw Hal mangled by farm machinery, thrown by his horse, choking on a bone with spilled wine spreading over a pure white tablecloth, his mother screaming for the servants. Or had it been bees? One time, when Hal and Ben had been playing on the grounds at Lachfahree, they'd disturbed a hive. The swarm stung both boys, but Hal ballooned up and turned purple, gasping for breath. Somehow, he'd survived that ordeal, but he'd been terrified of being stung ever since.

Wil shook his head, trying to rid himself of the traumatic images and return to practicalities. He was the third son. This wasn't supposed to be his lot, a lot made worse by his father's creeping madness. He tried to feel sympathy for his mother, with all the men in her life falling around her like wheat flattened by a thunderstorm.

Leaving only Wil.

The oft-forgotten youngest child.

The misfit.

He blinked into awareness of the pleasant warmth of the sun on his hair, the sound of geese squabbling in the distance. *Cloud Dancer* floated before him. Was it his imagination, or was there a note of sympathy in the boat's silent song? He drew a shuddering breath and let his eyes fall to the note, feeling the heft and quality of the paper between thumb and forefinger. His mother needed the best in all things. Wil snorted, thinking how disappointed she must be to be left with him. Her husband lost to madness. Hal, the practical one who could take care of her, lost to some unknown fate. Ben, who always frustrated her the most because of his wild fancies, but who was also her favorite. Now she would be reliant upon Wil, a child she'd largely ignored since giving birth to him. Or would she try to use him as a figurehead in order to run the family in his name?

Would he mind that?

Wil had never wanted to be saddled with the family name, fortune, or estates. He dreaded the responsibility and obligation that came with them.

Did he have a choice?

The words of the letter swam and blurred as he squinted at them.

"Hal has had an accident. You must return. The doctors say he might pull through, but even if he does, he will not be fit to run the estates."

What had happened to his brother?

"I have dispatched copies of this letter to all the towns along the canals near your last known location. Your little holiday jaunt is over. It is time for you to return home. Whichever solicitor finds you will have further instructions and funds to see to your travels. I will expect you shortly."

She'd signed the letter, Slirentha Billingray Cathermay-Gravence, Lady Breymerick.

Not Mother.

Of course not Mother.

Wil sighed and folded the letter, sliding it into his pocket. He needed to retrieve his suitcase and leave a note for the captain if she was still abed.

Should he check on her? Arrange for a doctor to visit, perhaps?

How long would it take to walk to town and find the solicitor?

He should probably change back into his school or traveling clothes and wash up a bit to prevent the solicitor's secretary from throwing him out on principle.

Wil stepped onto the boat.

And froze, thoughts tumbling.

How quickly he'd decided and with how little thought. He needed to go back, didn't he? Duty dictated what was expected of him, but...

He sighed again, head swiveling to take in the peaceful stretch of undisturbed canal. Only animals and the captain for company. The boat sang in his ears as if reminding him not to forget that it was also a living thing.

Wil shivered and descended the steps to the cabin.

39

She Wanted You to Find It

Wil hesitated as he entered the boat. Light streamed through the windows, but he knew he'd left the curtains drawn and bungs in place in the portholes last night. There was only one reason that would have changed.

The captain.

She sat on the cot, head down, cradling something to her chest. Her long braid had frayed and pulled apart. Wil's relief at seeing her awake tempered the frustration that he would have to talk to her. Would he have taken the coward's way out if it had been on the table, grabbing his things and slipping away from this aborted chapter of his life? Of course he would have. Guilt would have riddled him the rest of his life that he hadn't said goodbye, that he hadn't made sure she was okay. But certainly he would have slipped away quietly if he could have. Run away again. That chance was gone now. He swore he could feel an itch spreading from the letter in his pocket.

"Good morning," he tried.

She looked up, and he saw she had been crying, tears glittering in lines that seemed deeper now than yesterday.

"How long?" she asked, her voice raw.

"What?"

Her arms parted, revealing what she'd been cradling. The note-book. The journal of drawings and scattered words.

"How long?" she asked again.

She wasn't angry, but Wil couldn't place her mood more accurately than that.

He hung his head. "Since shortly after I came aboard."

"She wanted you to find it."

Wil's head snapped up. "She?"

"You hear her song. I've seen you listening."

"I don't—"

"You do. Not everyone can hear the Bound, boy. Not unless they have a gift or the Bound want them to. Which is it with you?"

Wil shook his head in mute confusion. The captain sighed and pushed up from the cot. It took her a long time to do so. She'd aged so much since he'd been aboard. Was that his fault, or was it the mysterious sickness she tried to hide? The captain carefully laid the notebook down on Wil's cot and put her palm against the paneled interior of *Cloud Dancer*.

She looked over her shoulder, eyes shining. "How much have you read?"

Wil's eyes tracked to the book. "It's not something you read, is it?"

The captain nodded. "True. It's more of an experience. But that was Karla."

Wil didn't ask who Karla was because he knew. He'd never heard the name before, but he'd been in her head, witness to her hopes and dreams, her meeting with the captain.

And the fateful fight with the crone.

"What happened to her?" he asked instead, knowing the answer yet not believing it was possible.

The captain looked away, pressed her forehead against the paneling. "Cursed," Wil thought she muttered, though he couldn't quite make out the word. Then her back straightened.

"Bound, as are we all."

Questions seethed in Wil's mind, but he dared not interrupt her.

He could see from her profile that her mind was elsewhere. If he said anything, it might break the spell.

"Karla," her hand waved about the cabin. "Her boys." Her hand dropped. "Me," she whispered.

Wil waited, the captain's silence like a storm building. Only it wasn't a complete silence. The boat's song was everywhere around them, and it felt strangely…comforting? But it was also troubling to Wil, and he needed to fill the awkward spaces, needed answers.

"The witch," he said at last, the words harsher and louder than he'd intended, and was a little ashamed to see the captain's entire body jolt in response.

She turned a red-eyed gaze upon him, tears worn without embarrassment on her weathered cheeks. One hand lifted to tug at her braid, fingers twining through the loose hairs.

"She ruined everything."

40

That Hurt was Honest and Good

Wil watched the captain's fingers toy with the ragged braid. They were long fingers. An aristocrat's fingers, meant for playing the pianoforte and cradling wine glasses. Though canal life had scarred and calloused them, their origins were undeniable.

He resisted the temptation to hold up his hand to examine his own fingers, the long and delicate digits scabbed and blistered from the unaccustomed labor of the past few months. They hurt, yes, but that hurt was honest and good.

Earned.

"We were so careful," the captain said, her voice nearly inaudible. "But the witch caught us. Probably one of the boys spied on us in the week prior." Her lip quirked at the corner. "Not that it earned them a reprieve."

Her accent and phrasing were shifting, abandoning the trappings of Rivane melody to fully embrace the precision and clipped tones Wil had grown up with.

Much like when she confronted the Harlebone boys.

"She pretended to leave for town but circled back behind the hedge that lined the towpath. I brought a picnic and a blanket so we could watch the balloons and spend a few stolen moments together, but Karla wasn't ready yet. I went into the boat. This boat." She glanced around, as if surprised to find herself there. "I grabbed her hand, insisting we only had a short time before the witch returned. Our fingers intertwined, and we had one last, precious kiss before the witch burst in."

The captain shuddered and sank in upon herself. "She was so small. Karla's boys were on the steps behind her, peering into the cabin, into the scene of their mother's disgrace. I thought..." Her voice trailed off, free hand rising to ward off a phantom blow. "I was shouting. Threats. Imprecations. Everything happened so quickly. There was a word the witch spoke..."

A shiver wracked the captain's entire frame, and she sagged against the wall, sliding down it to the cot. "I remember the witch's eyes. Black and glittering like coal. Her word brought pain like I'd never felt before, so much worse than falling from the sky and breaking my leg. I collapsed. Karla screamed. The boys were shouting. In anger at first."

A ragged breath. "Then the agony got worse. Splitting. Tearing."

Her fingers twitched, pulling apart the braid. She drew a stuttering breath.

The silence was smothering, thick like syrup. Even the boat's song faded. When the captain spoke again, her voice was a jagged whisper. Wil had to step closer to hear her.

"There was a tug inside me. Like a noose tightening." She yanked the hair of the unraveled braid taut with unexpected violence. "Binding me."

"And Karla?" Wil pushed the question into the void between them.

The captain lifted her blue eyes, eyes that Wil remembered looking into in his dreams, knowing that he loved her.

That Karla loved her.

"Bound," the captain hissed. "Their machines need souls to function. Many go willingly when their time is up. Others..." She shivered. "I touched Karla's hand. Still warm. But there was no life in her face or eyes. The witch had stolen her from her body, given her to the boat."

"But didn't the boat have a soul before? How else could it...?"

The captain nodded, her face twisted in a grimace. "The witch cast the previous soul out and Bound my love in its place." Her voice dropped. "And me to her."

Something bumped Wil's calf, and he looked down into three sets of amber eyes.

"And the boys," he whispered.

"Aye. She'd ordered them to keep away, but they were too curious and disobeyed her. They saw everything, and in the end they tried to save their mother. So the witch *rewarded* that curiosity and loyalty and sealed their young lips."

Wil's head spun. It was like a fairy story his nurse might have read to him as a child.

"We can leave her for a time, but the Binding is a leash. It pulls us back. All of us."

"Not me."

The blue eyes snapped up. "Not you," the captain agreed. "Not yet."

He could still leave. He should leave. It needed to be now, before she asked what he knew she was going to ask.

"I'm dying," she said.

Too late. Too late.

"And I don't want Karla to be alone."

41

A Narrow Channel

Wil walked until his legs went from merely aching to jellied, unfeeling appendages strapped to the bottom of his torso. Three times he walked the towpath between boat and town, crossing the bridge over the canal to Lower Misling, climbing past a three-lock staircase to skirt the edges of Upper Misling, and then returning to within shouting distance of *Cloud Dancer*. No sign of the captain. She must have returned to bed after her confession.

"I'm dying," she'd told him. "Where do you think I've been going during all these stops?"

He'd known, of course, or at least suspected, but he hadn't had the heart to contradict her.

"I may have been Bound to this boat, to these canals, but I am the last of an ancient and wealthy lineage. I have resources, and I've used them to consult every doctor I could find, no matter how old or inexperienced, how steeped in folk cures teetering on the edge of decency." Her head had dropped, voice shrunken to a husky whisper. "But it's eating me from inside, and nothing can stop it."

The blue eyes snapped up, bright spots of color in a colorless scene. "I can't leave her alone. She likes you. Always has. Probably why she gave you her journal."

Wil wondered how long the captain had been planning this. Had she known she was dying and saved him from his classmates for this very reason? How much of this adventure was of his own making?

How much had he just been a passenger and not crew?

It was just like the rest of his privileged, preordained life. The tutors, the boarding schools, the scheduled play with carefully selected companions. His own life was a canal, a narrow channel from which he could never deviate. How ironic that the one time he'd sought to break free from that routine, he'd chosen a canal, limited by its very nature, to escape on.

If escape he had.

If he'd even been the one to make the choice to run away.

He walked past Rivane boats, moored along the canal or navigating the locks, and felt his attention drawn to them, though he forced himself not to stare. How many of these boats and locks had the ghosts of ancestors, lovers, siblings, or enemies Bound to them? Was it all of them? How many non-Rivane knew their secret?

The fourth time Wil crossed over the bridge into Lower Misling, he made the mistake of glancing at a Rivane boat leaving the bottom lock. A girl sat at the bow, skirts hiked up over her knees and brown legs dangling above the water. She must have felt his gaze, because she looked up. Their eyes met and held. A smile of recognition tugged at her lips, and she nodded to him.

Wil's boot caught the edge of a cobble, and he tripped, staggering down the far side of the bridge. By the time he regained his balance and looked back at the boat, the girl had vanished. Had he imagined her? Rivane did not smile at him. They tolerated him. No matter how ragged his clothing or the honesty of the blisters on his hands, he was an outsider, not to be trusted. The illiterate might suffer him to read or write for them and lock keepers would accept his labor, but there was always a distance. Not deliberately rude, just an understood boundary between him and them.

Until that smile.

There had been recognition there, even a hint of acceptance.

How had that happened? Could the Rivane somehow sense his potential to be one of them now, to be wedded to a Bound engine?

Wil's deadened legs propelled him up the steps to Upper Misling. Lower Misling was the larger of the two sibling towns, sprawling along a flatland at the base of the staircase locks, while Upper Misling huddled beneath a hill at the top of the locks. The houses were older in Upper Misling, made of stone rather than wood. These were the shops and houses of whatever quality this provincial outpost could boast.

The solicitor's office would be on the High Street. Of that, Wil had little doubt. He felt unfriendly eyes on him, but didn't care. What did it matter if the people of Upper Misling judged him? He was beyond caring how dirty he was, how mismatched his clothes were. He just wanted…

Wil stopped dead in the middle of the street, conscious of being watched, his intentions weighed by invisible observers.

As he weighed his own desires.

What *did* he want?

He'd left Harlebone intending to hunt down Ben's widow, to find some closure for his brother's death. Instead, he'd spent months aboard a Rivane canal boat, running away from school, from family, from responsibility. And now…?

A family with only one heir remaining.

A captain with only one potential successor.

Wil was both, but he couldn't choose both paths.

He shivered despite the sun warming his shoulders, and a chill crawled up his numb legs and along his spine. His body jerked into awkward motion.

Find the solicitor.

Attempt to see him.

What matter if the man's secretary would likely escort him from the office before the solicitor knew of his presence? At least that would remove an option, a responsibility.

He wouldn't have to decide.

Wouldn't have to disappoint anybody.

42

Bowing to a Boy in Rags

The solicitor's secretary turned Wil away.

Of course he did.

The man's pale mustache had bristled with outrage as he glared at Wil's Rivane rags, sniffed as if Wil's mere presence brought a stench that invaded the office. Wil had been glad to shuffle back out the way he had come, but he hadn't gone far before the solicitor himself came stumbling out in pursuit.

He hunched before Wil, panting, hands on his knees, a bitter wind swirling scattered snow flurries around them. If the solicitor's struggles with the bicycle were any sign, he was not accustomed to physical exertion. Wil waited, glancing around to see what the handful of Upper Misling passersby thought of one of their august number gasping for breath at the feet of a dirty Rivane boy.

Eyes shifted away, though he caught some widening and others narrowing.

Polite folk in Upper Misling.

Wil bit back a smile as he thought of the web of rumors spreading from this encounter. What manner of trouble must they imagine the solicitor to be in?

When the man straightened at last, his eyes were sharp, though he mustered enough politeness not to glare. "You should have told me who you were when we met earlier."

The words fell somewhere short of accusation. Scions of great families were immune to such things from those who cared about their social standing.

Wil shrugged. If this man had suffered the indignity of a bicycle ride and an encounter with Rivane folk rather than sending his secretary, then Wil's parents were paying a hefty sum to get a message to him. Speaking of which…

"How did they find me?" Wil asked, dropping all pretense at being Rivane and mustering the cold disdain that was his birthright.

The solicitor blinked, startled at the incongruity of Harlebone-shaped words falling from the lips of a Rivane wastrel. "Excuse m-me?" He stammered.

"How did my parents find me, Mister…?" Wil pretended to have forgotten the man's name, though he knew it well enough from the letter. These were the little assertions of power Wil and his kind exercised. Though it felt strange and foreign, it was almost a relief for Wil to adopt such habits.

"Craine. Polidet Craine." The solicitor executed a little bow, and Wil fought down another smile. The good folk of Upper Misling would surely whisper behind their hands about this man of letters and law bowing to a boy in rags.

"How did my parents find me, Craine?" Wil left off the honorific deliberately, another assertion of power and privilege.

"I'm told that a schoolmate of yours saw you."

"Moske."

Craine shrugged. "The boy must have followed you, learned what boat you were on. When your school term resumed without you present, the masters set about hunting down word of your whereabouts. This boy provided the only confirmed sighting, so when your parents needed to contact you, it was simply a matter of finding the boat." Another shrug. As if it were nothing to command a small army to scour the entire canal network of Saxe-Colraine for a single boat.

"What do they want?"

"Yes, ahem. As I wrote…" Craine paused, eyes darting at the studied manner of others on the street, slowing as they passed but not looking in their direction.

He was clearly uncomfortable discussing such matters in public view, but Wil had no desire to allow him the shield of his desk and the armor of his law books.

Wil narrowed his eyes and held up a hand, wiggled the finger his family's ring would encircle when he became lord. "A matter of inheritance, I believe?"

"Yes, um, you see…"

"What happened to Hal?"

A frown. Was that because Wil had used his brother's informal nickname or because Wil's parents hadn't shared their eldest son's name with their hirelings?

"My brother," Wil clarified. "Halbern. The letter you delivered concerned him."

The solicitor paled and swallowed. "He's…"

"Dead?"

The man flinched as if the word had struck him a blow. His eyes went everywhere but Wil's face. Did he know Hal's fate or was he just guessing, piecing together clues from what little he'd been told?

"Accident with some farming equipment, I'm led to believe, though I do not have all the details. Nor do I know if he…"

Craine's hands fluttered, and Wil dropped his head to stare at the cobbles.

Had it been an accident or a deliberate act? Hal wasn't popular with his tenants and employees. Not that Hal would know. Such folk had always been beneath his notice. Ben had talked to them and had a particular talent for remembering the names of wives and children. He'd always been ready with a smile and a joke.

The solicitor coughed. Silly man probably thought Wil was grieving. As if he could feel grief over the fate of a brother who'd held Wil's head in a bucket of ice-cold water for over a minute when they were boys. As if he could grieve for a brother who hadn't written to him once at Harlebone. Not even a cursory note to check on his progress or to offer advice or support.

Wil lifted his head again and cocked it at an angle, forcing Craine to meet his gaze. "They want me back."

The solicitor nodded, hands clasped before him. "Of course they do. Funds can be drawn from any of the local banking houses…"

They wouldn't have bothered unless Hal was already dead or beyond hope. Wil wondered if they'd attempted to discover where he was before the accident forced them to call him home. Had they worried when he never returned home for break, or were they relieved he hadn't?

"Are you supposed to have the constables arrest me if I refuse to come?"

Craine's nostrils flared. "Refuse?"

"I'm not sure I want to be the fall-back plan."

The solicitor's frown was ugly. His tongue swept across his top lip. "You cannot…"

"Indeed?"

"But you are the heir now." Craine's hands danced, shaping some fictional landscape around them. "The grand house. The estates. Money."

Wil leaned his head back and squinted at the sky as if considering the man's words. There was much he could do with those things, of course, but they were their own sort of prison. Whereas the boat…

He frowned.

It was also a prison of sorts.

"You have papers for me, I suppose?" He spoke to the sky.

"Back in my office. Not the full lot, of course. Your family solicitors will have those, but I have enough for you to establish access to your accounts with our local houses, to fund a new wardrobe and transport back north." Craine paused, ran his tongue along his lips again. "Or to Harlebone. Or wherever else you desire to go."

Wil's chest prickled with cold. "I thought they instructed me to return to the estates. They'd let me return to school instead?" His eyes dropped to the solicitor, whose own gaze wandered, unable to meet Wil's. Wil wondered if he had children of his own and whether he shipped them off to expensive schools as well.

"I am sure they would prefer—"

"Enough. I know where to find you if I need you."

Wil spun on his heel and stalked off, leaving Craine spluttering behind him. He heard a few tentative footfalls come in pursuit, but they died off, and Wil increased his own pace.

Running away again.

43

You're Here for a Reason

Wil passed the bridge at the bottom of the staircase lock, feeling the momentary tug of *Cloud Dancer* calling to him, but he walked on instead, head down, kicking a small stone along the cobbles. Lower Misling had four mooring spots. The nearest two were occupied by a yellow boat and a red boat, while the third mooring was empty.

Denny's green boat sat alone at the fourth.

Wil passed the first two boats, wincing at the sounds of life within. Family sounds. Voices calling. Babes crying. Dogs barking.

A joyful tumult.

Denny watched him approach, viol cradled in his arms, long fingers dancing along the neck, wringing out yet another sad song. He nodded an invitation as Wil paused next to the plank that bridged the gap from cobbles to deck, but did not stop his song. Wil remained where he was, watching and listening.

The song wasn't complete.

Or was it?

There were gaps in what Denny was playing and singing.

Left deliberately for someone else to fill?

Wil closed his eyes and breathed. The distant throbbing in his head was always there, a precursor to another terrible headache. His father had complained of intense headaches as his fits worsened, and Wil had once overheard his mother speaking to a doctor about how they reduced his father to a shivering, weeping mess in his rooms at the sanitarium. Was this a preview of Wil's life to come?

The throbbing in his head fell into time with Denny's playing, and Wil slipped into the music, letting it wrap around him. Gradually, the puzzle fitted itself together, the song from Denny's boat filling the gaps left by his voice and viol.

Wil breathed.

How long had it been since he'd first heard them singing together? A week? Or more? That had been two distinct songs that somehow seemed to fit together. Maybe a coincidence. But this…

This was something more. A true duet with both singers feeding off and reacting to the other. Was it a different song or had something changed within him, making him more attuned to the boat's song? His foot tapped the cobbles, keeping time with the joined song, head bobbing.

He opened his eyes. Denny was staring at him, eyes going wide as he realized Wil wasn't marking time along with the viol but with the syncopated rhythm of the joined song. The tune wavered, lost the beat, then fell apart with a silent wail from Denny's wife.

"You can hear her," Denny mouthed. No sounds emerged, but Wil could read his lips. Denny shook his head, face pale. He found his voice. "You're not Rivane, not Bound. How can…?"

A hot flush stole over Wil's cheeks. He'd violated the man's intimate sharing with his wife. His eyes dropped to the cobbles. He shoved his hands in his pockets, pinching his thighs through the rough fabric, needing to feel something.

"I hear *Cloud Dancer* too," he said.

He heard Denny set the viol down and take a few steps across the deck.

"I think I could hear all of them if I wanted." Wil dragged a hand from his pocket and waved it vaguely at the canal. It was just a matter of concentration, of opening the haunted part of his mind.

If he returned to Old Garfo's lock, he knew he could hear what made the one-legged lock keeper weep.

Footsteps sounded on the plank, and Denny's shoes came into view on the cobbles. A gentle hand touched his shoulder.

"You're here for a reason, lad."

44

Still, He Hesitated

A decision was slow in arriving.

The fierce need from the engine prickled along Wil's skin, raising the fine hairs to an almost painful degree. But even that could not keep sleep at bay. He sank into a fitful slumber despite the rhythmic pounding on the inside of his skull, a hammer and anvil accompaniment to the serrated melancholy of *Cloud Dancer's* song.

Troubled dreams assailed him.

Fragments of a life.

Ben twisting to launch a smile over his shoulder, his scarf unfurling as the train crawled away, taking him to war.

To death.

Father behind his vast desk, frowning over papers, a tumbler of brownish liquid at his elbow, eyes twitching to the shadows. What did he see and hear there? Would Wil see and hear those same things as his own mind tore itself apart? Mother stood behind Father, prim and pale and proper, one protective hand on Father's shoulder as if she could keep him in the chair through force of will, keep him from slowly succumbing to the poison in his mind until she had no choice but to commit him to the care of professionals.

Committed.

Institutionalized.

The long dining table of the masters at Harlebone stretched before Wil, black-robed men like crows watching over the hushed ranks of silent boys eating.

Whispers in the dark from those same boys. Rumors of war. Boys of their station would never need to fight in such wars unless they were foolish enough to enlist or apply for a commission.

Foolish like Ben.

Then, like a balm, a plaster on the open wound of Wil's childhood…

The canal, stretching off into the uncertain distance. It reflected the open promise of the sky but caged it at the same time.

Wil woke with a start as something metallic clattered outside the boat. He shook his head, blinking gummy eyelids at the dead woman on the bed before him. He turned as a cat stretched nearby, yawning widely, showing its fangs. The boat rocked as someone jumped aboard.

A spark of panic jolted Wil to his feet.

Rivane boats were never locked.

Someone was shouting. A fist pounded on the door. Not Rivane. No Rivane would come aboard another's boat without invitation. Nor would they knock.

"Lord Breymerick! Are you aboard, sir?"

Not the solicitor, but someone sent by him, no doubt. Someone who had arrived via bicycle? Was that the clattering he'd heard before, a bike being discarded by the towpath?

"Lord Breymerick!"

Louder this time. More insistent.

Nobody knew he was here for certain. He could wait for the man to leave. Maybe the boat could make him leave? *Cloud Dancer's* eagerness washed over Wil, and he felt the tone of her song shift. The man on the far side of the door gasped.

What had she done to him?

"Lord Breymerick?"

The call was softer now. Uncertain and strained, issuing through clenched teeth. But something in that change made Wil realize what he'd been ignoring. The man was calling for Lord Breymerick, not Master Cathermay-Gravence.

Lord Breymerick was his father's title.

His eldest brother Halbern would bear it when his father died, which meant…

Wil stood, his muscles wooden and head pounding. He took one step toward the door and felt *Cloud Dancer's* eagerness, felt her grab something inside of him and drag him forward. Toward the engine. Toward her.

Panic surged like electricity along his spine. Had he been Bound without his consent? Had he made a decision without realizing it? Was he cursed?

No. He shook his head, feeling for the connection the boat was offering. He had not accepted. Not yet.

Another step and he was through the hallway and staggering past the cot where he had slept these last few months. Cats flashed past him, gray shapes in the gloom. He wasn't imagining them, was he? Wil paused in the galley, heard muttering and someone retreating up the steps. The boat rocked as the man leapt to shore.

Wil paused with his hand on the door handle, listening to the rattling of the bicycle being dragged upright. He heard a grunt and the sound of gears engaging.

Still, he hesitated.

Until a cat bumped his leg.

Wil pulled the door open, and an envelope fell into the boat. "Lord Breymerick" was scrawled on it in a fine, if hurried, hand. But Wil's eyes did not remain on the envelope for long. They lifted to find the hatch that concealed the engine.

And Karla.

Mother, wife, murderess, slave. Bound to this engine and this boat. Trapped. As the captain had been trapped.

As Wil himself might be trapped.

Here, or…

His eyes drifted back to the envelope. The black ink spelled out his future. He was a lord now. He could buy a hundred boats, cruise or sail wherever he saw fit to wander. On rivers or seas, in foreign lands or closer to home. Many nobles had similar eccentricities. It would be tolerated.

But not if he chose a Rivane boat.

Some things were beyond the pale for men of his station.

What would happen to *Cloud Dancer* if he just retrieved his suitcase and walked away, took a train to rejoin his family? What would happen to Karla? He did not know how the Rivane handled the inheritance of boats, but he knew Karla would not accept being Bound to just anyone. She would not be a slave again. If a new master tried to subjugate her, she would cause trouble. He knew this as he knew her. He had lived through her in dreams that were memories.

She wanted him to stay. Wil could feel little else but that need. It surrounded him and smothered him. Like he would be smothered on the family estates, chained to responsibility and ceremonies and tenants and…

Wil knelt, fingers brushing the envelope. Good paper. Not great. Cheap wax seal. But his eyes did not drop to study it. His attention fixed instead on the hatch that concealed the mystical engine and the imprisoned Karla.

Mother, wife, murderess, slave.

And partner, perhaps?

Wil drew a breath and made his choice.

Afterword

Sign up for the M.S. Hund newsletter to get the latest word on sales
and new releases plus exclusive content and free stories at:
bit.ly/mshundnews

THIS ISN'T THE CAGE YOU'RE LOOKING FOR

This book began as an attempt at using the Kishōtenketsu story
structure, but somewhere along the line it went off the rails and
crashed down into the familiar trench of western storytelling tradi-
tions. Talk about cages, eh?

Still, I'm happy to try something different, as I attempt to do
with each new project. The scaffolding for the next book is already
being erected, and, without spilling too much dirt, that story is going
to feature some interesting new architecture.

Returning, if I may, to the subject of cages, you may notice that
I no longer include links to Facebook and Twitter in the "About the
Author" section. Though those pages and profiles have not been
abandoned, I've taken a big step back from actively taking part on

social media, with the notable exception of Goodreads, which I use to track what I'm reading.

Follow along there if you're so inclined, or, if you'd like a more direct channel, you can always email me at mshund@mshund.com.

Thanks for reading!

- M.S. Hund

Acknowledgments

Special thanks this time to my younger daughter, Sylvie. This was the first book I've proofed by reading it to her over several nights as a bed-time story, and her reactions to several passages helped with some last minute tweaks I'm not sure I would have made otherwise. Thanks also to Jenn and Bella for their help in the editing process.

The image used on the cover of this book is courtesy Thành Nguyễn from Pixabay. A grateful tip of the hat as well to the development teams behind Scrivener and Vellum, whose software played a vital role in this book's production.

About the Author

M.S. (Michael Stephen) Hund is the author of the historical fantasy series, *The Dreambetween Symphony*. His other series, novels, and short stories run the gamut of speculative fiction from westerns to the occult to hard SF. Someday he hopes to live in a hobbit-hole with a well-stocked library and an equally well-stocked wine cellar. Until that happy day, you can make his acquaintance online.

www.mshund.com

goodreads.com/mshund

Also by M.S. Hund

The Dreambetween Symphony series

Song of the Severed Lord

Exile Ballad

Requiem

Preludes & Elegies

Tales of the Avernine series

Gunmage

Wardsmith

Revival

Purgatory

Demonhammer

Redemption

For a complete list of titles, please visit:

www.mshund.com